# BRIGHT MOON

# ALSO BY RON BRIGGS

**Yellow Hair Series**

*Erik Haraldsson*

*Tor's Saga*

*Cass*

*Westward*

*Journey to Iceland*

*Iceland*

*Redbone*

# BRIGHT MOON

## YELLOW HAIR
## BOOK EIGHT

RON BRIGGS

WOLFPACK
PUBLISHING
— EST 2013 —

**Bright Moon**
Paperback Edition
Copyright © 2025 by Ron Briggs

Wolfpack Publishing
1707 E. Diana Street
Tampa, Florida 33609

www.wolfpackpublishing.com

All rights reserved. No part of this book may be reproduced in any form or by any electronic or mechanical means, including information storage and retrieval systems, without express written permission from the publisher, except for the use of brief quotations in reviews. Any use of this publication to train generative artificial intelligence (AI) technologies is expressly prohibited.

This book is a work of fiction. References to historical events, real people, or real places are used fictitiously. Any similarity to real persons, living or dead, is purely coincidental and not intended by the author.

All brand names and product names used in this book are trademarks, registered trademarks, or trade names of their respective holders. Wolfpack Publishing is not associated with any product or vendor in this book.

Paperback ISBN 979-8-89567-153-5
Ebook ISBN 979-8-89567-152-8
LCCN: 2025932520

# FOREWORD

This is a work of fiction. The characters, events, and places are created by the author. Any references and actions by historical persons or places are fictionalized. An honest attempt has been made to describe real cultures and interactions as they may have taken place in the eleventh century CE.

So far in the Yellow Hair Series, we have followed Erik Haraldsson on his journey from wannabe Viking raider to responsible father, stockman, jarl, and shipbuilder. Then, followed his dream for a better life in the colony of Greenland. His dream is cut short by a horrendous storm that takes his life. His son, twelve-year-old Tor, is the sole survivor of two big knorrs that fall victim to that, and subsequent, storms leaving the boy floating on a plank in the middle of the ocean.

In the second book, Tor is washed up on a shore of a strange new world. He learns to survive and becomes a powerful young man. Then, word of his arrival reaches the burgeoning city of Cahokia, where a powerful chief sends the trustworthy trader, Traveler, to the east coast to bring Tor to Cahokia, where the chief can use his presence for political advantage. Before Traveler can find Tor, he is captured by an enemy of the Lenni Lenape People who adopted Tor. He must fight to escape his captors and return to his adopted clan. Finally, Traveler convinces him to make the journey to Cahokia.

The third book takes us back nine years to chronicle the tragedy and development of the courageous girl, Bright Moon. She received a message from a great spirit as her village was being destroyed and her parents savagely murdered. She was renamed Cass, and her twin sister was renamed Pena. Together they trained and pushed themselves until Cass was a honed warrior. Using unorthodox methods, Cass lured the evil war chief who orchestrated the destruction of her world into a fight and defeated him. After the fight with Thunder Throat, she found herself in Monongahela Village with no purpose and no future.

In the fourth book, Traveler and Tor stop at Monongahela Village where Tor and Cass cross paths. Love at first sight changes both their lives in profound ways. Cass decides to accompany the two men to Cahokia. The voyage is fraught with danger, but they finally arrive. In Cahokia, Cass meets old enemies and falls victim to deadly politics when she loses her baby early in her first pregnancy. Then, she learns she must fight a woman who has come to kill her. Tor is forced to participate in a funeral spectacle and play chunkey in a politically charged tournament. Finally, Tor learns from another trader that he may be able to find his way to a ship that will return him to his homeland.

The fifth installment in the Yellow Hair Series takes Traveler, Tor, and Bright Moon, formerly Cass, back to Monongahela Village, where Traveler decides to stay and settle down in the arms of the Head Matron. Tor and Bright Moon continue the perilous journey that takes them into lands controlled by the war chief who Tor had escaped from. Tor successfully leads the travelers to victory, and their journey continues. As they travel through the Lenape lands, Tor is able to catch up with old friends. After leaving familiar territory, they must continue on into the unknown. New perils are met and dealt with as they work their way to the Norse ship owned by Tor's great-uncle that will take the across the sea to Greenland, and finally, Iceland.

Book six tells the story of Tor and Bright Moon's life in Iceland. It turned out to be fraught with peril, just like their life across the ocean. But now they had to raise their five children in the turmoil of racial hatred as they struggled to navigate the Icelandic Norse legal system. In the end, Tor dies a horrible death from an infected cut he received while saving his young grandson from being trampled by a horse.

After Tor's death, Bright Moon, known in Iceland as Heidi, must fight off one more enemy before she drifts into a fantasy world, communicating with her twin sister far across the sea.

In book seven, we are back in the Monongahela lands catching up with Bright Star, Bright Moon's twin sister. Her first child is a son born with a deformed foot. The boy develops an unlikely affection for the former trader, Traveler. Growing up, the boy learns he is too slow and awkward to become a warrior and learns to be a trader. After meeting another trader, Redbone travels to the Lenape lands to learn about his uncle, Tor, who had been rescued and raised by those people. In a strange turn of events, he falls in love with Red Petal, whose life had been touched by Traveler when she was very young. Red Petal adapts quickly to the river trader life and goes everywhere with Redbone. Back in Redbone's home village, she meets his sister who is becoming a skilled hunter and wants to be a warrior like her aunt. Red Petal and Bright Moon become close friends before Redbone and Red Petal depart to trade their way to the Shining Mountains. A journey filled with wonder and danger. While in Cahokia, they witness the celestial event that triggers the growth of Cahokia to the largest city in their world. They also meet a trader that will guide them to the land of the Shoshone in the Shining Mountains.

Book Eight chronicles the life of Bright Star's daughter. She named the child after her sister, Bright

Moon, who had followed Tor to his world. Bright Moon was not like any other girl in the village. Her goal was to emulate her famous warrior aunt. As she develops into an adult, she becomes keenly aware of an increased threat from Haudenosaunee warriors who are becoming more aggressive with their probes and raids from the east. Bright Moon used her unorthodox mind to come up with new ways to defeat the enemy. She was able to prove to her war chief father that she was usually right. But the Haudenosaunee were still a growing threat. The evil Haudenosaunee chief sent his daughter to spy on Bright Moon to learn her defensive strategies. He planned an overwhelming attack on Bright Moon's village due to a vision he had. The attack came, and Bright Moon had to use every resource she could come up with, and a surprise she was not aware of, just to stay alive.

# BRIGHT MOON

BRIGHT MOON

# CHAPTER I
# WARRIOR

**B**right Moon carefully picked her way along the game trail a day's walk east of New Long Pine Village. She had seen ten and five summers and dreamed of being a respected warrior. She was born different from other girls. To her, clan duties entailed protecting her village and family from outside dangers and providing meat for her family, clan, and those in need. Decorated dresses, being courted by handsome warriors, working pottery, politics, and other trappings of clan matrons meant nothing to her.

This morning, her goal was to kill the big antlered buck she had gotten a glimpse of at the end of her evening hunt last night. It was the end of the Hunter's Moon, and the deer rut was in full swing. She knew this deer's territory, but territory meant little when does were running around wreaking in estrus. The breeding season would not last forever, and each buck needed to breed as many does as he could catch. Passing genes to the next generation was the most important thing a male deer had to do. More important than eating this time of year.

Bright Moon slowly worked along the trail to her ambush location. She was hopeful the big buck would be after one of the does that frequented the patch of witch hazel near the spring by the small meadow where she would wait for him to show up.

She reached her hiding place before the first hint of dawn dimmed the stars above. Slipping behind some screening laurel bushes, she found her log seat. From there, she had a good view of the witch hazel, the spring, the meadow, and far down the trail into the forest.

Many leaves had fallen from the oaks, maples, chestnut, elm, beech, and ash trees, giving her a good vantage for seeing far into the forest all around her. She should see her quarry long before he came by her hidden location.

While it was still dark, she strung her bow, stood it against a laurel bush, pulled three arrows from her quiver, and stood them by her bow. She was ready.

The stars above began to dim as the sky faded from black to gray to purple. The scattered clouds in the eastern sky took on the orange and pink hues of the new dawn. The shadows and shapes of the dark forest began to reveal their identity. Tree trunks, shrubs, leaves, rocks, and open spaces started to take shape as the sky grew lighter.

A movement caught her eye in the trees. *A doe. She is coming this way. Another and another. Soon she could see four does, including two yearlings, were coming her way. The breeze was tracking from behind the does and pushing to her right.*

All four does suddenly stopped, picked their heads up, and looked to the right. What looked like the oldest one curled its upper lip back and smelled the air. The breeze was at the doe's left shoulder, preventing her from smelling any danger coming from the right.

A twig snapped to the right. The does half lifted their tails but did not flee. All the deer looked in the direction the twig broke. One or another of the does moved its head in a circle trying to get a better look at the threat.

The monster buck made his appearance from the big trees to Bright Moon's right. He grunted and lowered his head, keeping his stretched neck parallel to the ground. He grunted again, and the two yearlings pranced back in the direction they came from. They looked back frequently and just sort of danced around, keeping an eye on the buck.

One of the does flicked her tail and kept it partially raised. The buck advanced toward the doe, emitting low grunts as he neared his target.

The buck never realized that he presented a perfect broadside view to a deadly predator with a sharp chert-tipped arrow ready to fly. Aiming just below and slightly behind the big deer's front leg,

Bright Moon let her arrow fly. The arrow penetrated deep into the animal's side. He jumped, threw his tail up, exposing a white flag, took two bounding strides, and collapsed on the forest floor. The does fled as fast as their bounding strides would carry them.

Bright Moon watched the buck carefully. Its front legs gave out first as the big animal crumpled to the ground. The back legs functioned for a few more heartbeats, then stuck out straight and quivered a few more heartbeats before going still. The chest was not moving and bright red blood oozed around the arrow shaft.

Slowly, Bright Moon stood and readied to go claim her prize, only two tens of paces from where she had sat.

Suddenly, another movement caught her eye. A buckskin-clad person was moving from tree to tree to the east and coming her way. Bright Moon slowly lowered to her knees and nocked another arrow in her bow.

As the warrior got closer, she could see well enough to know he was not from New Long Pine Village or Black Bear Village. Gradually, she was able to see his head clearly and knew it was a Haudenosaunee warrior. *What is he doing here? He scans the forest like he is looking for something, or someone.*

He kept coming closer but did not seem to notice her deer yet. He carried a strung bow with a nocked arrow. Now she could see red, black, and white paint on his face. He had three eagle feathers in his hair. Soon, he was in her range, but did not see her yet. She was well concealed by the gray-green laurel leaves.

When he spied the deer lying in the leaves with blood around its mouth and side, steam rising around the arrow shaft, he stopped and anxiously looked all around him. He looked as if he had seen two tens to two tens and five summers. He had several wolf track tattoos on his half-shaved head and forehead.

*What do I do? I do not know his tongue, so I cannot threaten him or ask what he is doing here. I could kill him easy enough, but...*

The warrior gave out a call, but he did not look back from where he came. He just looked around. *Surely, he knows whoever shot the deer was very close.*

He talked quieter. It sounded like a challenge. She did not move a muscle. He made what sounded like another challenge, then set his bow, quiver, and shoulder pack on the ground and pulled his belt knife. He stepped back and crouched in a fighting stance, holding his knife out in front of him.

*I am a fool,* she told herself. She set her bow on the ground, pulled her belt knife, and stood. Quickly she stepped out of the laurel bushes and got into a fighter's crouch ten paces from him.

His jaw dropped, then his mouth bent into a sardonic smile as he assessed his adversary.

"You know Monongahela tongue?" she asked, hoping he did.

He shook his head and started for her. She knew she had nowhere to go, so she stepped toward him. Suddenly, a change came on her. Her nerves were settled, all was quiet, and his motions seemed to slow. She could see that he was more interested in using her body than killing her. She also knew that her only chance was to kill him.

He charged and lunged at her, pulled his knife back and grabbed for her with his off hand. She slashed her knife up and across the underside of his forearm and jumped back. Blood gushed from his wounded arm. Shock, disbelief, and hatred shot across his face.

He knew he had to act quickly. He was losing blood fast and was in excruciating pain. But she was retreating too fast for him to catch her. His left arm was a bloody mess and his hand was numb. He drew back to throw his knife at her, but she was a moving target, and he could not focus. His head grew light, and he stumbled. Going down on one knee, he knew he was a dead man. Looking at his wounded arm, he saw blood pouring from the severed blood vessels. He grew weak and started to feel numb all over. His head started to weave, and he lost track of where the girl went. His vision started to fade. Suddenly, he felt his face hit the cold ground. *This cannot be...*

Bright Moon cautiously approached the warrior. He had dropped his knife, so she kicked it out of his reach. Blood continued to flow from his wounded arm as his breathing slowed. *Should I slit his throat. He is dying, regardless.* His body just seemed to relax, as if he were made of soft clay. She nudged his leg with her toe and got no reaction. Blood stopped flowing from his wound. She bent down and pulled him over. It took all her strength. He was definitely dead. *What do I do now?*

She carefully looked in the direction he came from. Nothing moved. *Surely, he was not here alone. Where are the other warriors? I need help*, she decided. She retrieved her bow, quiver, and shoulder bag and started back to the village at a trot.

By stopping only for a sip of water from her water skin and chewing on a piece of venison jerky while she ran, she was able to reach the Water Plant longhouse in New Long Pine Village shortly after the last light of the day was gone. Entering the big room where Bright Star, Red Hand, Water Mint, Tallow, Wise Beaver, Silver Star, Pretty Lotus, Longtail, Snow Lily, Green Hawk, and Oak Shield were just finishing evening meal.

"Unsuccessful day?" Bright Star asked.

"Pfft, hardly!" Bright Moon replied, getting her breathing under control. "War Chief, a word, please." She started for the back of the longhouse.

Red Hand followed her to her sleeping chamber.

"What happened that cannot be said to the Head Matron?"

"Nothing, but the others need not hear yet. Right after first light, I killed a big buck."

"You need help? Why all the secrecy? There is no shame in asking for help when you kill a big animal. But that *is* the reason most of us chose a partner to hunt with."

"If you are finished with your lecture and care what I have to say, you can stop interrupting me, Father." She struggled to keep her emotions under control.

"Well, what is it?" His tone matched hers.

"After the deer was down. I caught another movement far in the forest. It was a warrior. He was working his way through the woods on the same trail the deer used, but he was not looking for tracks."

"Who was it?"

She glared at him. "It was a Haudenosaunee warrior. When he got close enough, I could see he had paint on his face. Soon enough, he saw my deer laying in the leaves. The buck was only about two tens of paces from me, so I could not flee. He stepped over near my deer, set his bow, quiver, and shoulder pack down, pulled his belt knife, and called out what sounded like a challenge." She had his attention, then.

"For reasons I cannot explain, I did not just put an arrow in him." A pause. "I laid my bow, and quiver on the ground, next to my pack, pulled my own knife, and stepped out to accept his challenge."

Red Hand started to say something.

"Not finished, Father. If you like, I will tell this story to Mother, and you can leave the longhouse."

He crossed his arms and stared at her.

"The warrior was taken aback when I stepped out of the laurels I was using for cover. He laughed and gave me a lecherous grin. I just waved my knife in a circle, indicating I was ready for him. The fool smiled and shook his head. He was easy to read. He faked a lunge with his knife hand and tried to grab me with his left. As his open hand came toward my shoulder, I swung my blade across the underside of his forearm. He had a buckskin war shirt on, but my knife easily sliced to the bone close to his wrist. Less than a heartbeat later, blood was flowing from the wound like a river.

"He tried to chase me as I backed away from him. He soon faltered and dropped to his knees. In a few more heartbeats, his eyes rolled back in his pale face, and he toppled over. Shortly, he was dead. That is when I gathered my things and started for here to get some help.

"Surely, he was not alone, but no more of his kind came into my view. Believe me, I was looking for them until it was too dark to see. Now, I have a dead deer and a dead enemy out there in the forest. What should we do about it?"

"Why, in the name of all the gods did you chose to fight him? He may have dragged you back to his friends and who knows what would have happened to you!"

"We need you to be a war chief, not a doting father, right now. What are we going to do about the Haudenosaunee who are on our doorstep?"

"You are going to do nothing but stay in this house until I say otherwise. I will organize a party to go get your deer and see about the alleged enemy warrior."

"And you know exactly where to go? Would it not be wiser for me to lead you to the place. I could find it in the dark, blindfolded. Your party would fumble around in the dark, alert the enemy, and they would just fade away. You know I speak the truth."

He stood in silence for a few heartbeats. "Why must you always make things so difficult? Why can you not be like Water Mint's girls?"

"I was born the way I am. Are you going to do something, or should I talk to Mother? Maybe I should find a way to Aunt Bright Moon. At least we think alike." She turned and started for the firepit.

"Wait! Allow me to get my gear together." Red Hand had to admit, Bright Moon was right—she was always right about such matters.

Bright Moon turned to see her mother close by, but just out of sight.

"You heard?" Bright Moon asked her mother.

"I heard...and I am extremely proud of you. It takes courage to stand up to your parents...maybe more than facing an enemy warrior." She put an arm around her daughter.

"I never killed a man before. At first, I did not think I had hurt him bad enough to kill him. But he just lost too much blood, too quickly. I have not had much time to think about it. Now I feel a little queasy."

"Understandable. Sometimes there is no other way. You will be ten and six summers in a few moons. I was ten and seven when I killed a bad man. Your aunt was ten and six the first time, as well. Another question. You are surely a blooded warrior, now. Do you want the tattoos? I doubt they will invite you to the warrior's lodge, but I can arrange the tattoos if you like."

"Can I think about it until we return?"

"Of course."

––––––––

Bright Moon had the ten and five warrior party silently moving along the game trail long before daylight. Her plan was to come up on the deer carcass from the west. There they could move behind a low ridge where they could see if the deer had been disturbed without being seen.

She managed to get them into position silently in the dark. Red Hand was most impressed by his daughter's ability to lead these men. Some had seen more than two tens of sun cycles than she had.

Before the shadows began to disappear, she could see the deer was gone. Likewise, the body of the warrior was nowhere to be seen.

At first light, they moved in on the kill sight. It was easy to see where the deer had died, as well as where the man had bled out. The deer had been hung in a close tree to be butchered. The gut pile had been found by coyotes or wolves and was completely consumed. The deer skeleton had been stripped of meat and left on the ground, but the scavengers had ripped it apart. The skull was probably taken with the skin. *At least it will not be wasted.*

The man had been wrapped in a blanket and hauled away. It was hard to tell, but Sharp Nose, their best tracker guessed that there were at least ten warriors in the enemy party. They moved east when their job was done. Sharp Nose guessed that they had been gone at least eight hands of time.

On the trek back to the village, Red Hand took Bright Moon aside and praised her for the way she led their scouting party. He apologized for questioning her judgment and actions. He told her he would be proud to fight any enemy at her side. She decided not to take the tattoos—a stylized cattail plant on each temple for her first battle kill.

# CHAPTER 2
# MEMORIES

As she watched Redbone and Red Petal push his bark canoe into the current, Bright Moon thought of the changes in her short life. She had seen ten and seven sun cycles now. It struck her how both she and her brother had been so different than the other people they had known. She had never met anyone with a deformed foot like Redbone. Some elders said that it was not all that uncommon, but most children born with that deformity were taken into the woods before they were even washed and left for the animals. That was somehow supposed to be good for the baby and the family. Some went so far as to say that the creator saw those babies had a bad life soul and would become evil. That it was the creator's will that those babies be exposed. *Strange.*

*And then, there is me. Where do I fit in with the good souls and bad souls of this world. I have never been like other girls. Never wanted a cornhusk doll, never wanted to make pottery, or even plant the three sisters. Now that I am older, I never want to have a man. Nor do I want a woman. I have no desire to have feelings for just one person. I love my family, but I do not want one of my own. I love the clan, but I do not want any part of it, other than defending. The same goes for the village.*

*Now, Red Petal, she was different. We became such good friends while she was here. I never had a friend like that, boy or girl. Does that make my life soul bad? I do not know. Now, I just cringe when young warriors come around and want to court me. I can go out and hunt with any of them. I can practice combat and wrestle with them. But as soon as one suggests we touch or kiss, it just seems like my head fills with angry hornets.*

*Mother wants me to find a man, I know. She says she will not push me or make me marry someone I do not want, but I can see in her eyes that she wants me to marry somebody. I cannot. At least not at this point in my life.*

*What made me this way? Mother and Aunt Water Mint tell about the time, shortly after I began to walk, my brother led me around the longhouse. Supposedly I lost my balance and fell into the shit hole. I do not remember it, but Mother says Bone, later known as Redbone, saw me start to topple and caught my ankle just as I fell in headfirst. She says he pulled me out, but my head and arms, up to my elbows, were covered with the foul-smelling refuse. By the time Bone dragged me by the shoulder around to where the village women were pounding corn, I had both of us smeared with the stuff.*

*Water Mint claims it resulted in quite a laugh among the matrons. Perhaps that is why I never wanted a part in that life.*

*I remember, as a little girl, I was alone so much because I did not like to do "girl" things. I wanted to explore, find frogs, toads, salamanders, or big bugs. Most boys did not even want to do that. I wanted to hunt more than any boy ever did—and they are the hunters! I wanted to play stickball more than anyone else in the village. I still do—I guess that is why I am the best player in the village.*

*When Bone got hurt by a boy who bullied him, I just wanted to protect him. I think that is when I decided I wanted to be a warrior. I never had a friend in those days other than my brother.*

*But face it, the thing that gives me the most satisfaction is killing enemy warriors. Is it evil to want to kill men who want to kill you or your family? I do not have the answer. After that first one when I was hunting deer in the rut, I have killed three more. The only thing I feel is "there lies one more who will never harm my family." Am I evil? Maybe, but I do not feel evil.*

She found herself still standing at the canoe landing, looking downriver. *Do I want Redbone to come back? Or is it Red Petal? A problem with being a warrior is that when there is no one to fight, you get bored and frivolous thoughts make your mind wander to strange places. I find it hard to be "normal."*

She went back to her sleeping chamber and took up her bow and quiver and went out to hunt. She wandered somewhat aimlessly, wondering what Redbone and Red Petal would find in their wanderings. If it were not for the increased threat of the Haudenosaunee, she might have considered going with them. It was certain she would not find a friend like Red Petal in this village. *She is a one of a kind.*

*Redbone told me Traveler misspoke and said "Cass" when he was referring to Aunt Bright Moon. Corn Stalk changed the subject really fast. Later, Redbone asked Traveler about it. He only said the names "Cass" and "Pena" were connected to spirit power, and she forbid the use of either of those names in any Monongahela Village, clan, or household after the young women changed their names back to their childhood names of Bright Moon and Bright Star. I must ask Mother about that.*

When Bright Moon caught her mother alone, she asked her to walk with her. Bright Star could tell her daughter had something on her mind.

"What is the importance of the names 'Cass' and 'Pena?'" asked Bright Moon.

"Where did you hear those names?" Bright Moon looked around to make sure no one was within hearing range.

"Apparently Traveler used Cass in reference to Aunt Bright Moon. Corn Stalk was angered, and Traveler shut up really quick."

Bright Star's eyes glazed over, and she shook her head. "Those names are forbidden in this village," Bright Star barely whispered.

"Why?"

"Long story."

"I have time. What is it?"

"It goes back to *t-that n-night*. W...when our world was destroyed. W-we were t-there. In the t... tunnel, w-watching. He was raping and torturing our mother." Tears flowed freely from Bright Star's eyes, down her cheeks, and onto her tan doeskin dress. Her gaze was unfocused as she recalled the horrible night so many sun cycles in the past.

"And?"

"Bright Moon had her vision right then. She changed in a heartbeat. Gone was the cowering, crying, and frightened child. In her place was a calm, controlled warrior. From that moment until she ran off with Yellow Hair and Traveler, she dictated all our lives. She had a mission, and she compelled me, Aunt Water Mint, and Tallow to join in her vision and help her see it through. I gladly joined her cause—I had no idea what else to do.

"When we arrived in Monongahela Village, your aunt even convinced Head Matron Corn Stalk to not stand in her way. It was a strange time. A time of Power. Bright Moon was clearly guided by some mysterious spirit power. In her vision, she said Wolf, First Man, told her that our names were changed, that we would go by those new names until the task was completed, or we were dead. As you know, Bright Moon was able to do as Wolf told her she must."

"I still do not understand why those names were forbidden."

"Corn Stalk was always skeptical of Bright Moon's dream. But after Bright Moon did what she said she must do, the Head Matron became spooked. She thought there was too much spirit power clinging to Bright Moon and me. She associated those names with spirit power and felt it was just wrong to harbor it, and using those names was somehow going to keep the spirit power too close. I had already changed my name back to Bright Star, but Bright Moon waited until she married Yellow Hair in Cahokia."

"So, you were Pena?"

"Shush! Do not say that name out loud. Do not even think it!"

"It is just a word. What harm can saying it cause?"

"Please forget those names. We have enough trouble around in our family, clan, and village."

"I can never forget them, but I will not use them."

"Thank you."

As spring progressed, their enemies became more aggressive. Twice she had been called to the bastions with other archers to fend off warriors. Her aunt had planned the location of this village well. Any enemy coming from any direction would have to fight uphill to get to the palisade opening, and a path to the water supply was easily defended, making it nearly impossible for any enemy to lay siege to New Long

Pine Village. Because of the continued threat, Bright Moon volunteered to remain in the village with a contingent of warriors while many villagers went to the Summer Solstice Celebration in River Birch Village. She was relieved when the others returning after the big event were seen making their way upriver.

During the days the villagers were away, the palisade had been attacked twice. In those attacks, Bright Moon and her squad of two tens of skilled archers had killed more than four tens of enemy warriors. Both attacks had been repelled while losing only two dead and four wounded.

After hearing the news from the returning villagers, Bright Moon settled in for a good night's sleep. Her eyes were closed before her head laid on the blankets.

*It was a hot morning, and Bright Moon was sitting in a small thicket of trees. Enemies were approaching in a canoe up a small creek. She drew back her bow and sent an arrow into the first warrior's chest. Another was raising his nocked arrow when her projectile struck him in the throat. An arrow came from the side, and another dark warrior went down.*

*Suddenly a warrior was on her, swinging a warclub at her head. She ducked and swung her club up into his crotch. He went down screaming. She stepped out of her thicket. There was a warrior fighting Red Petal. Red Petal had been wounded. Bright Moon was quickly at that warrior's back, and slammed her club between the warrior's shoulder blades from behind. He went down, and the battle was over.*

*She wanted to help Red Petal, but she had to bury the six dead warriors first, but her feet would no longer move. Red Petal smiled and thanked her for coming. Then Bright Moon was walking up the hill to New Long Pine Village.*

Bright Moon awoke sweating and confused. She had obviously had a dream. Red Petal was there, but she never saw Redbone's face although she thought he was there some place. Had they been attacked? Had she just felt the danger? *Strange.*

At morning meal, Bright Moon told her mother about her dream.

"I told you how sometimes my sister and I felt what the other was feeling or, sometimes, thinking. You may have that kind of bond with your brother. Possibly even with Red Petal. You two seemed to have gotten very close since Redbone brought her here. I think they may have been in danger, and you felt it. The attack was probably real enough, but you were not there, of course. I think they must have fought their attackers off, and you were no longer needed. They must be safe, or your dream would have continued."

"If you say so, Mother. It could also have been just a silly dream. Do you think they will ever come back? Or will they live on the rivers the rest of their lives?"

"Oh, I have confidence they will come back,

someday, if they can. I want them to have children in this village. Just like I want you to have children in this village."

"You know that is not going to happen. I have no desire to be with a man long enough to make one, and I do not want to go through all things needed raise one."

"It is not too late."

*Yes, it is, Mother. You still do not understand just how different I am. I will never give you a grandchild.*

Five days after, the villagers, including her father, war chief of New Long Pine Village, allowed Bright Moon time to relax from constant guard duty. To her, relaxing meant spending time in the forest, hunting. She chose to cross the river and hunt along some of the creeks flowing into the Ohi-yo from the west.

The third night out, she was exhausted. She had killed a good-sized bear, and it was hard work getting it field dressed, skinned, fat stored in cleaned intestine sheaths, meat sliced from bones, and removing claws and teeth. In addition to all that, she had to make drying racks to get the meat drying over smoky fires.

She was ready for sleep when it became too dark to see. She thought she would plan her next day's activities but was asleep practically before she laid down.

*She was looking at a giant man-made mountain. It was almost as tall as the tallest trees. At the base of the mountain, there were crowds of people. They were all looking up the mountain to a flat terrace part way up. An older man in ceremonial regalia was talking to the crowd. At his side was a younger man in the same kind of regalia. While the old man talked, the crowds seemed to know what he was saying. Every so often they would yell out in roaring cheers.*

*She looked around, and Redbone was standing next to her smiling and pointing to something in the clear, blue sky. Bright Moon looked to where Redbone was pointing. There in the sky, on a bright, sunny day, was a star that shown as bright as any star shines at night. Everyone seemed to rejoice at the presence of that star.*

*Bright Moon tried to ask Redbone what it meant, but she could not make words. He seemed overjoyed and turned to Red Petal, trying to convince her of how important it all was. But she said, "Redbone, it may be important to all these people, but it means nothing to me. I want to leave here and go to the Shining Mountains."*

*"Then that is what we will do," he answered.*

Suddenly, a bright light shined into Bright Moon's eyes. She blinked and opened her eyes to discover the sun had broken over the hills and was shining in her face. Once more she was confused by a dream involving Redbone and Red Petal. *How can it be? What does it mean?* She decided to pack her bear kill back to New Long Pine Village and gift the meat and fat to her mother. She would keep the skin, teeth, claws, and enough fat for her own purposes. She had to wait another whole day for the meat to finish curing. That night she dreamed of Redbone and Red Petal paddling their canoe up a wide river lined with tall trees.

Upon arriving back in the village, she spoke to her mother about her dreams again.

"I just do not understand why I am seeing their lives in my dreams. What does it mean?"

"I think it means you and you brother have a close bond. I would not be surprised if he sees parts of your life in his dreams, as well. Do you wish to talk to Willow Bark about these dreams? She understands things beyond healing plants."

"Yes, I will go visit her."

Willow Bark invited Bright Moon into her firepit for a private talk over a cup of a special tea and acorn cakes. After sitting on tanned bobcat pads, Willow Bark filled a clay pipe with a substance from a yellow pouch she had taken from one of her baskets.

"I see you are wondering what is in the special tobacco in this pouch." Willow Bark in a soothing voice and a friendly smile on her face.

Bright Moon had had very little contact with the healer throughout her life. She could not remember being sick or injured badly enough to need a healer. And she could never keep her mind on the woman's soothing voice when she talked at various ceremonies through the sun cycles.

This day, the woman was in her shaman role, dressed in a blackened doeskin dress covered with black spirit symbol-stitched embroidery. Her mid-back length hair, streaked with a few gray and white streaks, was loose about her shoulders and hung down her chest. She wore a raccoon-like mask of black paint with three white streaks down each cheek. An obsidian bead was embedded in her left nostril. The shaman had seen three tens and five sun cycles.

Willow Bark gestured to Bright Moon to drink all of her tea and eat her acorn cake. When she was finished, the shaman refilled Bright Moon's cup. The first thing she noticed was the slightly bitter and unfamiliar taste of the tea. The cake had an ancient, earthy flavor. Almost immediately she had a warm, thistledown feeling in her head. Her vision blurred slightly, giving the shaman's smile a distorted, other-worldly expression. Rather than panic, she felt herself relaxing.

Carefully watching Bright Moon's reaction, the smiling shaman reached into the firepit and pulled out a burning twig. She held it to the pipe and drew air through it, lighting the tobacco concoction. The smoke was lighter gray than normal tobacco and gave off an acrid, but somehow soothing aroma. The shaman puffed to the four sacred directions, the earth, and the sky. Then she handed the pipe to Bright Moon and motioned for her to do the same. After the six puffs on the pipe, the fuzzy feeling grew stronger.

"How do you feel?" Willow Bark asked.

"Strange, but oddly relaxed," Bright Moon answered.

"Good. You wanted to talk about your dreams?"

"Yes. I have..." Bright Moon described, in more detail than she could remember, every aspect of the dreams she had experienced featuring Redbone and Red Petal. She felt herself transported back to the places in the dreams and feeling the sensations, even the sounds and smells of the action. It was more like living the dreams than when they occurred.

When she was finished, noted she was looking into the flickering flames in the firepit. She shook her head, and the fuzzy feeling left her. Her vision cleared, and her focus was sharper than when she was stalking a deer.

"Very vivid dreams, Bright Moon. There is no doubt you have experienced spirit dreams. The purpose or message seems unclear at the moment. But do not fear your dreams, the true meaning will come when your Spirit Helper decides you are ready. My guess is that your brother and his wife are reaching out to you for your strength in their times of trouble. You have remarkable inner strength. That is a gift."

"As long as I can remember my elders talking about her, I have wanted to be like my aunt, the one I am named for."

"Yes, she possessed the same kind of inner strength you do. I was still an apprentice when she left these lands, but I marveled at the things she did. I learned some of the plants with her. She seemed to know many things before our teacher ever opened his mouth. She could probably teach you things I cannot."

"I worry that my interests have driven me away from society. I am uncomfortable in large gatherings and cannot tolerate being around men who want to court or touch me. I do not understand that because there are good men in my life. As long as they are an honorable uncle or grandfather, I am fine. But as soon as some young man hints that he wants to talk about more than battle strategy, combat, or hunting, I panic and want to crush their skull. Am I evil?"

"No, you are strong-willed and young. You still have much to learn—about your feelings, your body, and your wants."

"I have seen ten and seven sun cycles. Most women my age are married and have children. Some are already widowed or divorced. I have never let a man touch anything but my hand. Furthermore, I have no desire for that to change."

"The same feelings your aunt had until Yellow Hair appeared, as I recall."

"Yes, well, there was only one of him. I doubt another will come along to prevent this Bright Moon from becoming an old crone."

"Like me. I have never known a man, you know. I have experienced intimacy with a few women, but I have never been drawn to have a long relationship with anyone. Some of us are just not born to be entangled with a partner. I would never be the healer I am with a husband—man or woman. You would not be the warrior you are with a man at your side to worry about, or a baby on your hip. I advise you to take life as it is, and if a man comes into your life someday, so be it. If not, accept who you are."

"Who I am, or what I am?"

"Meaning?"

"Sometimes ending another person's life seems like stepping on a bug. Does that make me as bad as those I kill?"

"There are many reasons to save someone's life. That is my place in life, and I find it fulfilling. There are also many reasons to take someone's life. Many of those reasons are justified. There are many evil people in the world. Only you can decide who is to live and who is to die when you are looking down your arrow shaft, wielding a knife, or holding a warclub. Not all enemies must die, and not all friends must live. Trust yourself to make the distinction but do it with a clear conscience."

"Thank you, Willow Bark. I feel better."

"You are most welcome, young war leader. I pray you find peace throughout your life."

"Could you tell me what you put in that tobacco?"

"Not a chance." With a smile, the shaman turned and walked to the back of her lodge.

## CHAPTER 3
# BULL HEART

Dancing Bull came into the lodge. He had taken a bath and put on a clean war shirt with quill decorations, a new breechclout, and leggings. He approached the bedding where Red Petal was bound. As he moved away from the light of the fire, his features became darker.

"Will you release my bonds, Chief?" Red Petal boldly asked.

"Will you fight?"

"Would you, if you were in my place?"

"I like a fighter." He gave her a sardonic smile backed by the confidence that he could do as he pleased. If it was lighter, she would have seen the bulge in his breechclout.

"Are you an honorable man, Dancing Buffalo?" She purposely left out the "Chief" to show she considered him just a man.

"I am Chief, address me as such! I am the most honorable man in this village," he proudly announced.

"I asked, Chief, because, among my people, forcing a woman, even a captive is considered very dishonorable. Only the weakest of warriors rape the women they capture. And the offense can be punishable by death, to be carried out by the offender's clan."

"Why would I care what your people do? You are a ripe cow, and I will mount you."

"So, you are a dishonorable man?"

He slapped her so hard, her ears rung and little lights danced in her eyes. "Your insolence will only bring you pain!" He quickly removed all of his clothing.

She grimaced when she saw his very large manhood at full erection. *He is even bigger than Redbone.* With her hands tied behind her back and legs bound at her knees and ankles, she felt helpless. *I cannot stop him. Tears leaked from her eyes. I will not cry out. I will not react in any way.*

Then, the big man bent down to untie the bindings on her ankles and her knees. With her knees free, he yanked up the light sleeping dress the women had put on her. He pulled the front of the nightdress over her head and bunched it behind her head. She thought she would be able to kick him, but her legs were numb from being bound for the past two hands of time. She could only give in.

The chief brutally entered her and pounded into her like a bull elk in rut. His hard squeezing of her breasts made her want to flinch, but her only reaction was the shedding of tears that trickled from her eyes. He never even looked at her face. Finally, he grunted like his namesake and pumped his seed into her. His hot stream seemed endless. She lay motionless.

"You are a useless bitch! I give you to my wives to cook for their lodge!" He got up, grabbed his clothing, and spit on her before walking to the other side of the lodge and laying with his three other wives.

Red Petal stung where he had ruthlessly drove his manhood in and out of her. It was no more than him exerting his control over her. She was too uncomfortable to sleep, and no one came to offer her any assistance. Throughout the night, she shifted and tried to relax enough to sleep. But her shoulders burned from having her hands bound behind her back, and her arms were dead numb. The bunched dress behind her neck strained against her skin felt like a dull knife cutting into her. *The worst night of my life. But I must stay strong for Redbone.*

When the smoke hole in the lodge began to turn gray, Meadow Dew came to Red Petal. "You need to get up and get the fire going. The women will expect you to make tea and warm up last night's stew. Are you well enough?" the young woman whispered. She rolled Red Petal onto her side and cut the thong binding her wrists. Her arms fell limp, but she could not feel them. Meadow Dew helped to her knees and massaged the feeling back into her arms, bringing pain. After she could feel her arms, she started flexing her fingers, causing more pain. Eventually, Meadow Dew helped her to her feet.

"Can I empty my water anywhere?" Red Petal asked, dreading how much that would hurt.

"I will lead you there. They seem to trust me."

Red Petal limped along behind Meadow Dew toward the latrine at the edge of the camp. A few other women appeared, apparently with the same goal. Meadow Dew was not finished with her urination when a Comanche woman grabbed her arm and yanked her away, urine splashing down her leg.

"Real humans use the piss hole before Shoshone snakes!" the woman declared.

If Red Petal had any more strength, she would have kicked the woman, but her own urination had burned her irritated woman parts so much, she was trying not to collapse. She tried desperately to hold back her tears. Gobs of Dancing Bull's seed continued to ooze from her tormented woman hole down her shaking legs. She prayed this nightmare would end soon.

Redbone and Sheep Talker were having their own issues. The guards posted to watch them tied their arms around pine trees and left them standing. If they tried to relax, their shoulders had to bear their entire weight. They spent a long, cold night while their guards lay sleeping in snug buffalo robes. The morning brought no relief. The guards awoke and rolled out of their robes. They looked at their prisoners, decided they were going nowhere and walked away.

Redbone looked around at what little of the camp he could see. The most obvious thing was just away from them were about three tens of buffalo hides stretched and staked out on the ground. The hides were flesh side up and were in various stages of being scraped.

Wood smoke began to fill the air as morning meals began cooking. It smelled as if everyone was having buffalo stew. Redbone and Sheep Talker had had nothing to eat since the previous morning, and only one mouthful of water. Redbone wanted to just lay down and sleep, but his arms and shoulders hurt too much. *Red Petal has been with that brute all night. I am sure he violated her. She may have resisted and been killed. I could not save her. This is all my fault. Never... should...brought...her...*

Pronghorn Hunter ran into the camp on the north side of a hill just north of the Flat River. Bull Heart had been waiting for him since the sentry announced he was coming in nearly a hand of time past.

"What news have you brought, Pronghorn Hunter," Bull Heart called out when the man was twenty paces away.

The young scout had seen ten and seven summers. He was the fastest runner with the keenest eyesight in Bull Heart's village. The weather had been chilly overnight, but not freezing. The snow of the previous morning was already gone. He was covered in sweat and huffing like a buffalo run to ground. Dried sand clung to his bare legs, wet breechclout, and bare chest.

"Dancing Buffalo has his lodges set up in Antelope Valley, and it looks like he plans to winter there." Pronghorn Hunter bent over with his hands on his knees and talked between ragged breaths.

"He knows we always set our winter camp in that valley. What is his strength?"

"Pronghorn Hunter counts four tens and five warriors old enough to take up weapons and fight. There are probably three tens of women and small children and less than ten elders. They have racks of buffalo meat being dried and smoked. They must have caught a herd in the valley."

"Thank you for that detailed report. Go get some food and rest."

"One more thing, Chief. Dancing Buffalo captured two trader canoes yesterday. One appears to be that of your Shoshone friend, Sheep Talker, and his daughter, Meadow Dew. I do not know the other man or woman."

"Woman?"

"She and the man wore plain buckskin shirts and leggings. I could not identify their nation. They looked young, but I could not get very close. It seemed like some of Dancing Bull's rear guards spotted them on the river, then set up an ambush to capture them. I did not see either of the women this morning."

"This is an outrage. I think we will go teach Dancing Buffalo a lesson in manners."

Within a hand of time, Bull Heart and his nine tens of warriors were on a war walk to Dancing Buffalo Village in Antelope Valley. The war party was crossing the river in less than another hand of time. They were moving up Antelope Creek when one of Dancing Buffalo's scouts spotted them and ran to the main village.

Redbone heard a shout. Suddenly, the entire village was in action. Women and a few children were herded toward the trees high on the northwest side of the valley by five warriors. It looked like Red Petal and Meadow Dew were among that group, though it was hard to tell because of the distance and his situation.

Shouts and confusion seemed to rule the day. Warriors ran past Redbone going one way, then, were soon running back the other. Eventually, Dancing Buffalo had his men together and were retreating southwest up Antelope Creek. Redbone and Sheep Talker were left to fend for themselves.

Within two fingers of time, a warrior came running up to Redbone and Sheep Talker. The warrior cut the ropes binding them to the trees, and they both fell to the ground. The warrior started to give Redbone water as others arrived. Redbone did not know whether they were friends or enemies, but he knew he was grateful for the water.

As soon as Redbone could gather his thoughts, he yelled, "Red Petal! We must save Red Petal and Meadow Dew!"

"Who is Red Petal?" the warrior who seemed to be in charge of the ones rescuing Redbone and Sheep Talker.

"My wife. They took her to those trees up there." He frantically pointed to the trees where the women and children had fled. Lifting his arm to point up the hill felt like he was lifting a buffalo with one hand. He could see now they were trying to work their way toward the creek where Dancing Buffalo was leading his retreat.

Bull Heart arrived on the scene and told his men to pursue the escaping warriors.

The women and their escort seemed to be moving slower than they should have. From a distance it appeared they were arguing in several factions. Finally, an aggressive-looking woman went up to another, who seemed to be struggling with someone who appeared to be tied to her. The aggressive woman pulled what looked like a knife, made a slashing movement, and the one who seemed to be struggling fell to the ground and lay still while the other fled.

Redbone panicked, assuming Red Petal was the struggling woman and was now dead. Then he saw that the party of Bull Heart's warriors was closing in on the fleeing women. Redbone started hobbling that direction, but his sore and exhausted body would not allow him to make much progress.

Now, Bull Heart and three others were tending to Sheep Talker, who was still unconscious.

Redbone looked up the hill and saw the woman he thought was Red Petal was sitting up, apparently talking to one of the warriors. A movement down the hill near the creek distracted him. A young woman was running down the creek bank, looking back frequently. A party of Bull Heart's warriors reached her, and she collapsed at their feet. When he looked back to Red Petal, she was gingerly coming down the hill with the help of one of the warriors. Apparently, all of Dancing Buffalo's warriors had escaped.

Red Petal and her escort neared where Redbone was drinking water and eating some pemican in an attempt to recover. He could see the pain etched in her face with each tentative step.

"Wife, my heart sings to see you alive." He struggled to his feet and hobbled toward her.

"Husband, thank the creator your life was spared. I feared the worst." They embraced, more holding each other up more than anything. "Are you hurt badly?" she asked, looking him over as best she could.

"I will live. But how badly are you hurt?"

"The injuries will heal, my husband, but the terror in my heart will take some time. I am damaged in more ways than skin and bone."

"My precious wife, I should never have brought you here. I am so sorry. It is all my fault." Tears filled his eyes as he held her gently.

"Stop that talk right now! I will not have you taking blame for something you had no control over. Do you hear me? No blame! I need you to be stronger than ever. We can get through this, but only by helping each other. Tell me you understand and that you will not blame yourself from this moment on." He hesitated. "Tell me!" A pause. "Tell me or leave me right now! We cannot wallow in it! Tell me!" she screamed as tears filled her eyes, and she shook from head to toe.

"I will not blame myself," he said weakly.

"Mean it! Please, I need your strength," she blubbered.

"I will not let you down. Do you need some medicine? Anything for the pain?"

Redbone looked around. Warriors were milling around the abandoned village like ants around a kicked anthill. He held her arm and urged her toward the village where her nightmares lived.

"W...where...y...you taking m...me?"

"We need to find you some medicine. Elm bark or willow tea, at least."

"I...ca...cannot go t...that village. Please do not m...make me go t...there."

"Night will come too soon. There is nowhere else to go."

"Just hold me. Be my man. Take care of me." He held her.

Sheep Talker had recovered somewhat and, with help from Meadow Dew, hobbled over to Redbone and Red Petal. "Are you well, my friends?" the older trader asked.

"We will survive. Thank you for asking, elder."

"Bull Heart tells me our canoes are untouched. At least we have our supplies. His warriors and whole village will be here tomorrow. He plans to set up his winter camp at the fork of Antelope Creek, about a day upstream from here. What do you wish to do tonight?" Sheep Talker looked around for a place they might set up a temporary camp. He had heard Red Petal say she could not go back to the village. He could not blame her. That site was tainted. It was too far to go back to the river and get their own camping gear, and anything here would be out of the question.

Redbone looked at the many buffalo hides stretched out on the ground. Yes, they were green and might smell some. But they were shelter. By tomorrow, Bull Heart's men would have their canoes and gear up the creek, and they could all feel better.

That night, as Redbone and Red Petal lay awake, wishing they could sleep, she began to cry.

"I could not stop him, Redbone. My legs were bound for two hands of time. He just cut the bindings and took me. I could not stop him. I wanted to, but I could not. I tried to shame him for raping a captive. It seemed to make him more aggressive. I am so sorry! I c...could not s...stop him." She turned to cry into his shoulder. He kissed her on the top of her head and hugged her to him. She cried for a finger of time before she fell asleep. It took him much longer. When he was confident she would not awaken, he wept for her.

*She will be a long time getting past this. I must be strong for her.*

Morning brought a gentle southern breeze. The sky was cloudless. Ordinarily it would be one of those days to get a lot done. Things as they were, Redbone and Sheep Talker were too sore and weak to do much of anything. Couple that with Red Petal's pain and lack of desire to do anything, and they were in trouble. They had much hard work to do and had no ability to get it done. Meadow Dew stayed with them to keep them in fresh willow bark tea and buffalo stew.

Bull Heart's warriors were told to leave the meat on the drying racks and keep the smoking fires going. They were instructed to let any of Dancing Buffalo's warriors who came back to retrieve their winter food supply and whatever they wanted from the old village, to let them have it as long as they left in peace and stayed away from Antelope Valley for the winter.

Most of Bull Heart's warriors were gone to help his village in their move to Antelope Creek Fork. Only seven warriors remained, scavenging through the deserted Dancing Buffalo Village for anything of value.

Redbone was staring up the hill where the women had fled with Red Petal and Meadow Dew as prisoners. He wondered what had transpired up there but was not about to ask. Red Petal was sitting still, breathing slowly, while she stared into empty space. *She needs time.*

A movement caught Redbone's eye. Along the creek came Dancing Buffalo with ten and five warriors and ten women. They were dragging travois poles, and he carried a white arrow. Redbone let out a loud "whoop." Bull Heart's warriors came at a run, stringing bows and nocking arrows. Dancing Buffalo raised the white arrow over his head. Redbone noted that none of the Dancing Buffalo warriors carried strung bows.

The parade of warriors and women stopped at least five tens of paces from Bull Heart's warriors, who had spread apart but kept their arrows nocked.

"Dancing Buffalo comes in peace. These warriors are here to assist the women packing our village to move to another winter camp. We ask only that we take what is ours and will leave this place."

"Bull Heart demands that Dancing Buffalo leave Antelope Valley for the winter," Elk Runner said without emotion.

"Dancing Buffalo will winter on Lodgepole Creek. Bull Heart and any of his warriors are not welcome there."

"Then gather your things and leave. Bull Heart is not responsible for anything his warriors may have scavenged from your abandoned village. Note the meat racks are untouched. He would not deprive even you of your winter food supply. And your buffalo hides are left for you to take. Gather all you can, for you will not be welcome back. Also, while you are here, you will keep your distance from these traders. Elk Runner, Second War Chief of Bull Heart Village, has spoken!"

Dancing Buffalo quietly talked to a few of his warriors and turned back to Elk Runner. He brought his right fist down into his left palm, indicating "Good Trade." The women went into lodges to see what they could salvage. The men began unpinning the green buffalo hides and dragging them to the meat smoking racks. When they left, they had taken most of the buffalo hides and smoked buffalo meat. All of the lodges had been dismantled. The coverings and poles served as additional travois. Every man and every woman, except Dancing Buffalo slipped into a harness that fit over shoulders and a padded band on the forehead to drag a travois. They would have a long day before they could enlist the help of their fellow villagers who were more than a day south of them.

Red Petal quivered in Redbone's arms the entire time Dancing Buffalo was in the vicinity. She refused to stand and walk down to the creek. She did not want him to see her stand on trembling legs.

Long before Dancing Buffalo's party left the abandoned village site, the first of the Bull Heart warriors began to arrive. Pronghorn Runner and three other warriors paddled Redbone and Sheep Talker's canoes up the creek from where they had been left two days prior. That brought a smile to Redbone's face.

It was late afternoon when the last of Dancing Buffalo's party disappeared over the hill south of Antelope Creek. Red Petal turned her face to Redbone and pleaded, "Husband, please take me to the creek. I must wash that foul man from my body and my souls."

Redbone was elated that she showed some sign of life. Together they hobbled down the gentle slope to where the canoe was tethered to a willow bush. Redbone dug out a drying hide and some soapweed he had for trade. They walked around some screening bushes and began to disrobe.

Red Petal pulled off the light-colored, thin pronghorn skin sleeping dress she had been given, and threw it in the creek. She did not care how comfortable it was, she would never let it touch her skin again. When she pulled it from her legs, she noted the pink area where she had leaked onto it while sitting down. That brought a flash of *That Man* rutting in her. Tears came to her eyes.

When Red Petal pulled the dress over her head, Redbone was appalled to see the deep bruises defacing her beautiful breasts. In addition, the big bruise on her face was beginning to darken. Anger filled his heart. He gimped over and wrapped his arms around her. His own arms screamed in pain from the simple movement. She put her face into his neck and shoulder and cried.

"I do not wish you to see me like this, my husband. I am so ashamed."

Hot tears flowed down his naked chest. It was the first time since he had known her that he held her naked body without being aroused. He pitied her for what she had been through and wanted to comfort her, his own lust put on a back shelf somewhere.

Together they separated and slowly stepped into the creek. The water was cold, but far from freezing. They were quickly submerged to their necks and working the soapweed into a soapy lather. She found the cool water soothing to her damaged woman parts, but the soapweed burned the raw flesh. Finally, she just sat on a submerged rock and let the water flow over her.

Redbone found another rock he could sit on. They just sat there in silence for a finger of time. The shadows were getting long, and camp was still not set up. He started to rise, but she put a hand out to stop him.

"I want to love you, my husband, but I...I...c... cannot right now. That cuts my souls. No husband could be better than you. Thank you. Thank you."

"No woman can match your strength, and the

love in your heart is my world." They stood, embraced, and made for the creek bank.

They were drying the last of the water from their skin when Meadow Dew stepped around the bushes.

"I saw you two down here and got jealous. I put a stew together and have some fat heating up. I have some biscuitroot flour. I am going to make some frybread for evening meal. I hope you do not mind me intruding on your private bath. I thought it would be better if I did not remove my clothes where the young warriors could watch. They have too many wild ideas as it is."

"You are always welcome, my friend. I just do not want anyone to see this bruised body." Red Petal began to weep as she put on a buckskin shirt, loin-cloth, leggings, and moccasins.

Well after dark, members of Bull Heart's village came straggling in with heavy burdens of lodges, meat, hides, and personal belongings. The next day they would arrive at the forks of Antelope Creek and set up their winter encampment.

Redbone marveled at how fast and efficiently the women put the village up. Pole frames were first, followed by skin coverings. Each dwelling had its own painted identity depicting family history or some major event. When completed, the lodges stood about two man-heights tall, with a smoke hole at the top and a flap for a door. They covered a circle about two tens of hands across. Soon, a firepit appeared in front of each lodge, with a bigger one near Bull Heart's lodge which was nearly twice the size of any other in the camp.

Redbone and Sheep Talker planned to set up their camp close to the village by the creek. Bull Heart interrupted them and said they were guests in his lodge until they move on in the spring.

# CHAPTER 4
# FEELINGS

A few days after her talk with Willow Bark, Bright Moon was awakened by a call from a sentry that a scout was coming in and was in a hurry. She was dressed in her red war shirt, bristling with weapons, as she rushed for the longhouse door hanging. She was two steps behind War Chief Red Hand. Tallow was following, still stowing weapons in their proper places.

They were near the palisade opening when the scout came through. Bright Moon did a quick check to affirm archers were at the ready on the catwalks on the palisade walls. More archers were joining their ranks as the scout came to a stop, propped his hands on his knees and addressed Red Hand.

"War Chief! At least ten-tens of Haudenosaunee warriors are headed this way. They wear war paint, carry ladders, and many carry bows. They are less than two hands east of the village." The long report had him gasping for breath.

"All warriors to your stations! Women bring water for the walls, prepare food for our warriors, make room in each longhouse for wounded. Bright Moon, take command of your archers. This will be a long battle, aim well."

Bright Moon scurried up the ladder to join her squad of archers. "You all know the routine. Aim to wound as many warriors as possible. Every wounded man needs attention. Any dead man is a source of arrows, so aim to wound. Shoulders and upper legs if you can. Post along the walls and shout out enemies approaching. Make sure the water bags are distributed along the catwalks, but close to the wall. We do not need anyone tripping over a carelessly placed water bag."

She worked her way along the catwalk patting warriors on the back, reassuring them she was there with them. When she reached the end of her squad, she asked the first warrior in the next squad if they had everything they needed. On down the line everyone waved at her. They all knew she was the best person in the village with a bow, and it was comforting having her among them. By the time all six tens of archers were in place and ready, Red Hand and Tallow had ranks of warriors lined up close to the walls to fend off any breeches in the palisade or to stand in for fallen comrades.

All too soon, Bright Moon could hear the unmistakable sound of warriors working through the thick forest. When she established this location for New Long Pine Village, Bright Moon's aunt, the first Bright Moon, had warriors come out and cut a swath of trees five tens of tens of paces from the walls. She had them fall all but the straightest trees and leave them lay haphazardly on the forest floor. The straight trees were used in the palisade. In the ten and nine sun cycles since, the swath had become a tangled mess that would slow any attacking army trying to fight their way to the village.

The strategy was on full display as the Haudenosaunee warriors hacked away at the jungle of saplings and rotting tree trunks in their path. The anxious warriors cursed and yelled as they tried to hurry their way through. Many were becoming frustrated and demoralized as their hard work seemed fruitless.

In previous attacks, the warriors were able to follow trails the village hunters used, but that would concentrate their numbers too much for an attack of this scale. Now, there were warriors standing around waiting along the hunting trails while the bulk of the fighters battled their way through the tangled barrier the brilliant woman had conjured all those sun cycles past.

After a hand of time battling against the forest with little progress, the Haudenosaunee war leaders called off the attack and faded back into the eastern forest. Some fights were too costly. Once again, the absent Bright Moon proved to be a worthy opponent.

After the enemy had retreated and the warriors gathered in the plaza, Red Hand cautioned them not to be complacent.

"The enemy is resourceful and determined to gain our hunting lands. We cannot let our guard down because of this one victory. Keep practicing and maintain a sharp edge on your weapons and your minds."

Later, at evening meal, Bright Star looked satisfied.

"My sister continues to amaze, even after being gone all this time. I think she is smiling right now, knowing this village is safer because of her efforts. And not just her, but all who worked so tirelessly to make that barrier possible, even though they knew it would take many seasons to fulfill its purpose."

Bright Moon smiled, thinking that one more of her idol's crazy ideas proved itself. *I have a long way to go before I am as brilliant as she was at my age. But I feel closer to her than ever.* Bright Moon went to sleep with a satisfied smile on her face.

*It was a brilliant day. She was in a bark canoe on a strange river in a strange land. There was a mix of bunch grasses, some grayish leafed brush, and green trees on the higher hillsides. In the distance, mountains appeared. Some looked like they had patches of snow near the tops. She was following a canoe with a young woman and an older man. She did not recognize the cut of their clothing.*

*They rounded a curve, and there were five warriors pointing arrows at them. She turned, looking for an escape. When she turned back, she was walking next to the young woman along a trail with a rope snugged around her throat and others behind her.*

*Then, they were in a lodge. It was dark and hard to see. The only light was from orange coals in a central firepit, but she was bound, back away from the fire. A big man ducked into the lodge. He looked around and came toward her. Arriving at her bedding, he bent down and freed her legs, but she could not move them.*

*He stripped his own clothes off and pulled the front of her dress over her head. She did not understand. Then he forced his huge manhood into her. She could do nothing as he rutted her mercilessly. His ugly face became imprinted in her memory. Finally, he released his seed with a deep grunt, like a bull moose.*

*Next, she was sitting on a hillside near a creek. She felt like she had mounted one of the tall, thin pine trees that seemed to be everywhere. Then she saw that man's face, larger than life. He smiled like he had just won a game of painted pebbles. She did not understand, but she knew she hated him.*

*Suddenly, she was in the middle of a ring of onlookers yelling in a tongue she did not comprehend. She had a knife in her hand. The dirt underfoot was smooth on her bare feet, and her only clothing was a soft loincloth.*

*That evil man stepped into the circle. He was totally naked, and his huge manhood was erect. Sweat glistened on his tattooed chest, arms, and face. A spiral tattoo on his face was interrupted by a deep scar.*

*He charged her, slashing with his big knife. She ducked away and prepared for the next attack. He came, faking one way, then twisting another. She barely avoided his blade. His moves and attacks were vicious, but she narrowly escaped each one. He came in low, and she jumped over his outstretched arm. She slashed down leaving a bloody gash in his shoulder.*

*His arm dropped as she landed on her feet just past him. She spun around to see him switch the knife to his left hand and charge after her again. Sidestepping, she slashed at his wounded right arm. Her cut barely broke the skin. He stepped back, assessing what to do next. Blood was flowing down his arm from his shoulder wound.*

*He raised his knife high, let out a blood-curdling war cry as he brought the blade straight down at her. She froze. The obsidian blade glistened as it approached her face...*

She shot to a sitting position, sweat pouring from her entire body. It was pitch black. *What did that mean?* She trembled as the adrenaline slowly drained from her blood.

"Red Petal is in danger!" she said aloud.

In three heartbeats, her mother was at her bed.

"What is it? Are you well?" Bright Star asked in a worried voice.

"It is Red Petal. I think she was raped by an evil man. I think Redbone is a captive, and they are in the

Shining Mountains. It was horrible. I felt her being raped, Mother. How can that be?"

"I know not how you could ever know. They could be anywhere. We will have to wait until they return."

"In my dream, I was Red Petal. At the end, I was fighting that man to the death with knives. I damaged him with deep cuts, but at the end, his knife was coming down at my face, and I could not stop it. Has she been killed?"

"What of your brother?"

"I do not know. I had the feeling that he was there, but I never saw him."

"I think you have just had a nightmare from all the stress you have been under with these Haudenosaunee raids. Perhaps you should take some time for yourself. Do whatever you like for a while. You know, coupling with a desired partner is a great way to relieve stress. There are several candidates in this village, or Black Bear, or anywhere else. You are a very attractive young woman. Warriors would fight over you anywhere you go," Bright Star suggested.

"We have talked about this, Mother. I have no desire to find a desirable partner. One does not exist. Please leave that topic alone." Bright Moon felt her stress increasing. She finished her tea and went to her sleeping chamber. Moments later, she returned with her bow and her waist belt bristling with weapons. "I need to go kill something," she said as she passed her mother sitting at the head of the firepit.

Bright Moon went down to the canoe landing, took the one-person canoe she frequently used, and paddled downriver. Around midafternoon she returned to the landing with a large buck deer that had started shedding the velvet from its antlers when she ended its life. The work of field dressing it, then dragging it for over two hands of time had her ready for a bath and a good night's sleep.

[faint mirrored text from previous page bleeding through]

## CHAPTER 5
# MORE RAIDS

A fter telling the story to Red Hand at evening meal, Bright Moon went off to bed early. A dreamless night and uninterrupted sleep, she awoke refreshed and ready to face the new day. The sun had not yet topped the hills to the east when a scout came in to report another Haudenosaunee raiding party was advancing through the forest toward New Long Pine Village.

Following their practiced routine, they were soon at their stations awaiting the enemy. This time the raiders followed established trails through the slash, then spread out to form a several-pronged attack formation.

Bright Moon was the first to launch an arrow at the enemy archers. She had built a new bow according to directions given by Yellow Hair to Red Hand and Tallow. It seems that in his homeland, they used longer, stronger bows that would shoot accurately much farther than the common hunting bows of this land. She had practiced at length from the palisade wall and knew just how far she could accurately shoot an arrow from that elevated perch. Then she had trained all the warriors under her control to build those bows and do the same.

The raiders were under the impression they were out of range and were forming their ranks before advancing into range of their own bowmen. They were totally surprised when a hail of deadly projectiles rained down on them. Ten of the forty warriors in that formation went down before they knew they were under attack.

The raiders, however, did not retreat. Instead, they charged as fast as they could run. Bright Moon and her trained squad shot arrow after arrow into their midst. But concentrating on the threat rapidly charging toward the palisade, they missed the second wave forming to attack while the advance unit withered under Bright Moon's defenses.

With the first wave was steadily losing numbers, Bright Moon began to wonder why they had not retreated. The few remaining kept coming, though they had no chance of making it to the palisade. She looked back to the forest where to first group had formed to see twice that many formed up, ready to advance.

She did a quick count and noted they had greatly depleted their supply of arrows. Then she realized the enemy's strategy. They would come in wave after wave, sacrificing warriors to deplete her ability to fight off the second and third wave.

Bright Moon yelled down to her father that they needed more arrows, and to be ready to repel enemy warriors storming the palisade. Quickly she refilled her quiver from the baskets of arrows stored along the catwalk.

She turned to her station just in time to see a rank of enemy archers loosing their arrows at her squad along the palisade. She ordered everyone to duck. With the noise of battle raging, not everyone heard her. Five of her ten and eight archers took arrows to their upper torsos. Three were fatal.

As soon as all of the incoming arrows landed, she stood and launched her own. Her ten and three remaining fighters followed her lead. They shot, and ducked again, as the second volley of enemy arrows was on the way. Avoiding any more casualties, they slowed and eventually stopped the second wave.

As the third wave started toward them, Red Hand's men were bringing new baskets of arrows up to the bowmen on the catwalk, who were beginning to run low.

The enemy was shocked that the New Long Pine defenders continued to send wave after wave of arrows accurately into their ranks. The third wave faltered and failed to make any headway at stifling the defenses of the village.

Finally, the raiders withdrew and called off the attack. Under a truce, they were allowed to gather their wounded and retrieve their dead from the battlefield.

Of the ten and eight warriors under Bright Moon's command, three were wounded and would recover from shoulder injuries. Three others were killed outright, including a young woman who emulated Bright Moon. Three more villagers were killed and five wounded while defending other sections of the palisade.

Bright Moon spent the afternoon consoling the families of her dead warriors. It was especially difficult talking with the mother of the young woman who was killed. The mother was widowed when her husband was killed in one of the earlier raids. The girl killed was her only daughter, and she had planned to get married during the fall equinox celebration. The distraught mother blamed Bright Moon for her daughter's death.

"You knew she wanted to be just like you. You put her on that wall and led her to her death. Get out of my lodge!" Sitting Dove told Bright Moon. What could she say.

Well after dark, Bright Moon finally crawled into her blankets. The rape nightmare came to her again. This time, she was not killed but made a slave. Each night the evil chief would come to her blankets and take her, except it was her eyes in Red Petal's body. Bright Moon did not feel the pain, but the humiliation was undeniable. She woke up crying and bathed in sweat long before first light. When she tried to get back to sleep, the image of that ugly chief came to her. Sleep was impossible. She got up and had sassafras tea brewed and sat by the firepit until the others stirred.

"Reliving the battle?" her father asked.

"No. A nightmare about something else."

"Care to elaborate?"

"No."

Then Hopper was there, and the subject changed when he asked Red Hand about going out and finding arrows from the battle.

The Green Corn Celebration coincided with the fall equinox, but the festivities were subdued after Sitting Dove's daughter had been killed and the wedding canceled. A bright spot was when Hopper received his adult name of Oak Shield during his naming ceremony. All of Water Mint's children were now adults. Six days after the equinox, Bright Moon woke up feeling sad. She knew of no one in the village who was sick or close to dying, yet she felt that someone very important had gone on to walk the Path of the Ancestors.

At morning meal, she shared her feelings. Both her mother and aunt said they also felt some kind of a loss that they could not name. After a long discussion, no conclusions were made.

Five days later, Fast Hawk arrived at the landing in a one-man canoe. His long face portended bad news.

"My heart cries to tell you that the Beloved

Trader has gone on to the Ancestors. We all miss his amazing stories," said Fast Hawk.

"Is there to be a funeral?" asked Bright Star, a tear trickling down her cheek.

"Head Matron Corn Silk ordered the shaman to clean his bones and store them in the House of the Dead. A great funeral and feast will be part of the Summer Solstice Celebration in Monongahela Village in the coming sun cycle. She wants the word to spread and expects a huge crowd."

"I wonder if there is a way to get Redbone back for that," Bright Moon said absently.

"Use your dream power to tell him," Oak Shield offered.

*I could take a one-person canoe, and…no, the deceased trader talked about the winters in the Shining Mountains. I would have to wait until the Planting Moon, then would not have enough time to get out there, find him, and get back for the funeral. Too bad.*

"New Long Pine Village will do all we can to help the Head Matron make the celebration of the trader's life a success. Thank you for bringing this mournful news to us. We needed to hear it," Bright Star told Fast Hawk.

# CHAPTER 6

# BLACK BEAR VILLAGE

" I must carry the news to Black Bear Village, too. When finished, I would ask that I may stop here to rest," Fast Hawk pleaded.

"Of course. This is your home. You are always welcome in this village," Bright Star replied.

"I will assist with your journey to Black Bear Village, if you do not mind," offered Bright Moon.

Everyone looked at her with questions in their eyes. *Twelve days and nights, just the two of them? Could she be coming out of her shell?* No one dared speak the obvious questions.

"Uh, I guess it is all right." Fast Hawk tentatively answered, looking at her family members with just as many questions as they were mulling over behind their eyes.

Seeing what was happening, Bright Moon quickly added, "You need not be concerned about anything of an intimate nature taking place. My

60

motives are strictly concern for my brother and the Beloved Trader."

Mixed reactions spread among her family members.

By early afternoon, Bright Moon and Fast Hawk were paddling a two-person dugout upriver.

"You should know that I am no longer married to Green Lark." Fast Hawk confessed as soon as they were around the first bend in the river.

"Oh?" she encouraged him to elaborate.

"She missed her moon soon after we were married. Then, a moon after that, she started with the morning sickness. But it got worse, quickly. After a restless night of much cramping, she found she was bleeding...down there. She lost the baby. She became hateful to me, blaming me for the loss of her child. I did not know what to do to make her return to her old, loving self. It was like her souls were loose. I went hunting with Strong Elk to help him if he killed a deer. With his leg still healing, he would need help if he was successful. When I returned to the Deer Clan longhouse, my belongings were outside the entry. A moon later, she was married to Hunting Fox. She now carries his child in her womb." Fast Hawk's voice was filled with melancholy.

"Sorry to hear that, friend. What will you do now?" she asked innocently.

"I do not know. At first, I thought you asking to come with me to Black Bear Village was a thinly veiled invitation, but I think I, and your clan, read your actions wrong."

"You are right. It was no invitation. What I want is any information you might have about where my brother and his wife were going. Second, I need to find out how the Black Bears are handling the increasing Haudenosaunee aggression."

"I know you are a dream beyond my reach, but I have to tell you, you will always be welcome in my camp."

"Well, you can forget about your camp. I am not interested in your, or any warrior's, advances. I have other, more pressing issues to be concerned about. But I could always use another warrior in my squad. We lost three dead and have three more still recovering from injuries from the last raid. So far, we have kept them out from the gates, but they keep sending bigger raiding parties and trying new tactics."

"Do you think my clan and my family would welcome me back?"

"I cannot answer for them, but you are a member of the Hawk Clan. That should be for life. You did nothing to get outcast for. Last I heard, moving to another village to be with a wife's clan is expected. I can see no issue. But I do not have a seat on the Hawk Clan council."

"My father was the most upset with me."

"Fathers are always upset when their offspring do not do what they expect. I cannot understand that either. Your father's responsibility ended when he sired you. How you turn out is up to your mother and uncles, not your father. It took me some time to get that through my father's thick skull, too. Now we are good friends, and he respects me as a warrior. Of course, I had no uncles in the village to teach me. Father wanted me to become a meek little clan maiden. That was never going to happen—too much of my mother's and aunt's blood running through my veins."

"You family is remarkable. My grandmother talks about what a great leader your grandmother was. And of course, your mother and aunt are legendary. Even your brother has far exceeded everyone's expectations. I am honored to call him friend."

"There is a good campsite just around the bend up ahead. The shadows are saying it is getting about time to put in." Bright Moon used her pointed paddle to indicate where the campsite was. "The best place is on the west side of the river. There is a natural canoe landing over there and a small hill with a little clearing."

They were sitting on each side of the often used fire ring at the edge of the clearing she pointed out. The sun had set, and it would be a cool night. They were both dressed in buckskin shirts, breechclouts, leggings, and moccasins. Bright Moon wore a buckskin headband with no beadwork to keep her long black hair from her face. On the lonely river, she did not worry about braiding or putting her hair in a bun to indicate her status. Fast Hawk wore his hair in two braids that hung down the front of his shirt.

Although it would be cool overnight, Bright Moon did not see the need to set up a shelter. She had elk and deer hide robes that would keep her warm enough. Fast Hawk was so used to setting up a small shelter that he did so without worrying about what she was doing.

After a meal consisting of corn gruel with chunks of dried venison and sassafras tea flavored with mint beebalm flowers, the light was fading fast. Bright Moon announced she was ready for some sleep.

As he was crawling into his small shelter, Fast Hawk said in a teasing tone, "Now you stay out of my tent tonight!".

"That I can promise you. And you will be much healthier if you never made such a remark again." Her reply left no wiggle room for him.

The clear morning had barely turned the blackness to gray shadows when Bright Moon whispered into Fast Hawk's ear. "I broke my promise—I sneaked into your tent. You had better get up, dressed, and ready for action. We have company— four Haudenosaunee scouts are just up the river from here."

"What? Who? Where am I?"

"Shush, or I will club you myself. They are still sleeping. They arrived deep in the night. Apparently, their leader did not think a guard was needed. If we do it quietly, we can eliminate them so they will not be able to report our strength on this side of the river, which is none."

"Wait, you want to just sneak over and bash their heads in without talking? They might have information we can use against their war leaders."

"Maybe we will keep one alive until he talks. We need to move before they wake up. Let us get at it."

"You are cold."

"Yes. Come on."

When they got close to the enemy camp, they had started to stir. One was coaxing a small, nearly smokeless fire to life. One was off taking care of his personal ablutions. The other two were rolling up bedrolls. Bright Moon spied the one coming back to the camp. He was just out of sight of the others when she loosed her arrow. It found its mark at the base of his throat. He dropped without uttering a cry. The arrow went through his larynx before shattering a vertebra and severing his spinal cord.

Although the warrior made no sound, the twang of Bright Moon's bow alerted the others. The one bent over, working on the fire yelped, but by the time he stood and reached for his own bow, her second arrow drove into the left side of his chest. The arrow nicked his sternum and deflected through his heart. Hitting the bone absorbed enough energy that the arrow did not protrude from his back. He staggered and fell, clutching at the bloody shaft.

Fast Hawk was shocked that Bright Moon shot the warrior who was still arranging his breechclout, then, a heartbeat later, was launching another arrow with pinpoint accuracy into her second target. He concentrated and fired an arrow at one of the warriors at the bedrolls. He was just reaching his bow when Fast Hawk's arrow slammed into his side. The angle carried the arrow through his intestines and plowed into his upper lumbar vertebrae. His spinal cord was not severed, but the shock temporarily paralyzed him. He dropped to the ground screaming.

The fourth warrior just wrapped his left hand around his bow as his right was pulling an arrow from his quiver, which was leaning against a tree. Bright Moon's chert-pointed projectile sliced through his left forearm. The arrow went between the ulna and radius, barely slowing down before sticking into the ground several paces away. Blood flowed from the entry and exit wounds.

"Drop to the ground!" Bright Moon demanded. He did.

With nocked arrows, Bright Moon and Fast Hawk approached the two warriors they knew were still alive. The other two were obviously dead. The one Fast Hawk had hit in the belly was weakly trying to staunch the bleeding around the arrow shaft protruding from the left side of his gut. The blood was dark and smelled foul. He knew his life was over.

Much to Bright Moon's surprise, Fast Hawk talked in very passable Haudenosaunee.

"What is your name, warrior?" Fast Hawk asked.

"Runs the Wind needs a healer, fast," the fading man answered.

"No healer can save Runs the Wind. Where is your village?"

"Ganeco Town."

"Why are you raiding on the Ohi-yo? The Mud River flows through great forests full of game. Surely you are not in need of hunting grounds."

"Our chief, Skanatego, son of Ganeco says the destiny of our people is to rule all the land south of the Long Lakes. We will control everything between the Ohi-yo and the Lenape Rivers."

"Why are you west of the Ohi-yo?"

Runs the Wind cramped and vomited a large clot of black blood. His eyes rolled in his head, and his body fell limp. "Maybe we can get more from that one," Fast Hawk looked to see that Bright Moon had tied the warrior's good arm tightly to his thigh and had put a tourniquet below his left elbow.

"He is all yours. Where did you learn to speak the Haudenosaunee tongue?" Bright Moon asked.

"I picked up a few words from various captives over time. But mostly, after I said some word in that tongue in Monongahela Village, the Beloved Trader took it upon himself to teach me. He said it might become useful sometime in the future. I guess he knew what he was talking about."

"Mother said he always did seem to know more than anyone else. I will let you see what you can get out of this one. He is not going anywhere. I will go pack up our camp and bring the canoe up here. We need to be moving—we still have more than four days travel."

The wounded warrior refused to provide any information to Fast Hawk. He told the man it was hopeless. The other one had told him Skanatego's vision, and why they were being so aggressive. When the last living scout provided nothing useful, Fast Hawk told the man the woman would kill him. He called Bright Moon a worm-eating snake who fornicates with tree roots.

"What information does he offer?" Bright Moon asked when she walked up from the river.

"None. I even told him you would kill him."

"So be it." She took up her waist knife and cut the tourniquet from his arm. Then she cut a piece of rabbit skin, rolled it to form a fist-sized ball, and forced it into his mouth. Finally, she sliced across his wounded arm to get the blood flowing faster but not gushing.

She pushed Fast Hawk to the riverbank where she had parked their canoe. They remained quiet until they camped that evening.

"Do you think that one we left is dead yet?" Fast Hawk asked tentatively as they sat by their small fire that night.

"Probably. Since I am here, and he is there, I cannot say for sure."

"I never knew you were so cold."

"That is a good reason why no man should try to court me."

"What made you so bitter? If I may ask?"

"Not sure I am bitter. But I have been in many battles with those people lately. I am cold toward them because they have started a war with us. War is a cold business, and if you are not cold, you and those you love will be dead, or worse. I feel a duty to protect my clan and our people. As for being cold toward men, I simply do not need the distraction. I may never. I am going to get some sleep now."

Bright Moon put up her small shelter that night. Thickening clouds filled the western sky as the sky darkened.

Morning broke to a cold, foggy mist. They packed everything up, protecting as much as they could from the wet air. They pushed north in miserable quietness. The birds and squirrels were silent. The mammals were hunkered in holes and burrows while the birds were puffed balls of feathers hidden in the fall-colored canopies of the bigger trees.

Occasionally they munched on dried venison, jerky, or pemican. Vigorous paddling was the only way to keep from freezing, so they worked hard at it without talking. The mist stopped midafternoon, but the temperature did not rise, and it remained cloudy and gloomy—just like their moods.

Fast Hawk tried desperately to conjure some way to melt Bright Moon's cold heart. He even fantasized about making her his wife. *By the gods, getting in her sleeping robes would be a dream come true.*

Bright Moon's shoulders, arms, and hips were aching when she slid into her bedroll in her tent that night. Sleep came fast.

*Bright Moon found herself sitting cross-legged by a fire ring in a round lodge with double skin walls. The orange and yellow flames gave off the distinctive scent of burning cottonwood. To her left sat Red Petal, Redbone, a young woman who looked familiar, a man who may have been her father, and more people she did not recognize. A big man looked at Redbone and asked if he is still sorry his trade brought him to this country. Redbone looked at Red Petal, and they both smiled without talking. But she leaned over and kissed Redbone on the cheek. All the people in the lodge smiled.*

*"It was hard getting past what that man did to me, Chief, but thank the Ancestors, Redbone stayed by my side and loved me through the pain. I feel like a woman again."*

*"It is good," said the chief.*

*No one seemed to notice Bright Moon. She stood to leave the lodge.*

*Redbone turned to look at her. "Thank you for checking on us, Bright Moon. It means more than you think."*

*"I need to tell you, Redbone, the Beloved Trader has gone to live with the Ancestors."*

*"Yes, I know. His spirit came to visit me."*

*"Of course, I should have known he would. I should*

*go now—I have a long way to go. Fast Hawk is waiting for me."*

*"Fast Hawk waiting for you? What of Green Lark?"*

*"She divorced Fast Hawk and married someone else."*

*"You and Fast Hawk?"* Red Petal asked in a hopeful voice.

*"Nothing like what you are thinking. We are on our way to Black Bear Village to deliver the news about the Beloved Trader and to discuss the war with the Haudenosaunee."*

*"I am confident you will defeat them."*

*"I can only pray. What of you? Are you coming home anytime soon?"*

*"When the winter is over, we will follow Sheep Talker and his daughter, Meadow Dew, to the camp of Tall Ram in the Shining Mountains. As hard as this country is, we are in a land of plenty, sister. We may never want to leave. You had better leave before the snow binds you here. Thank you again for coming...*

"Are you coming? It is light out, and the river is waiting," Fast Hawk called from outside her tent.

"Yes, I will be right there. But I need to take care of my personal needs before we shove off." Bright Moon was suddenly in a better mood. *Because of the dream? It seemed so real...*

As they worked their way north throughout the cloudy day, Bright Moon told Fast Hawk every detail of her dream. Some parts over and over again. He was curious about what Red Petal said about "that man." She explained how a past dream showed Red Petal being taken by an evil chief.

"You never fail to amaze me," Fast Hawk said.

"Do not go there, Fast Hawk, you will only be disappointed."

"I know, but I can still dream."

"Yes, you can still dream, just make sure it never gets past the dream stage. And if you keep making remarks, your dream will turn into your worst nightmare. Agreed?"

"Agreed." She was in the front and did not see the frown on his face.

Just past the middle of the following day, the Black Bear Village palisade came into view. Before they got within a hand of time from the landing, a canoe with five warriors pulled close to them.

"Who are you and what business have you in Black Bear Village?" the young warrior in the front demanded.

"I am Bright Moon of the Water Plant Clan and daughter of the Head Matron of New Long Pine Village. I am here to discuss matters with the Head Matron and War Chief concerning the Haudenosaunee. This is Fast Hawk of the Hawk Clan who is here to deliver news from Monongahela Village."

"I have never met you, maiden, please accept my apologies for being overly cautious. We have had our own problems with the Haudenosaunee. My name is

Flat Deer of the Deer Clan of Black Bear Village. I am the son of Head Matron Cool Dawn and War Chief Ten Point," the warrior politely stated.

In Cool Dawn's longhouse, formal introductions were exchanged. At Bright Moon's suggestion, Fast Hawk passed his news. A discussion followed about what a great and intelligent man the Beloved Trader had been. Black Bear Village pledged any assistance they might provide for the funeral during the Solstice Celebration.

Cool Dawn wore a highly decorated, light-tan-colored doeskin dress and ropes of various sized shell and bead necklaces. Her dark-streaked graying hair was braided and wound around the top of her head and held in place with deer bone skewers. Crow's feet surrounded her dark eyes and full lips. Though she had seen five tens of sun cycles, she had lost little of the beauty of her youth.

"A special treat tonight, guests. My son killed an elk on his morning hunt. This evening's meal will feature fresh-roasted elk meat," Cool Dawn announced.

Among the guests at the Head Matron's firepit was Goldeneye, Black Bear Village Matron of the Duck Clan and adopted mother of Red Hand, Bright Moon's father.

"My heart sings to see you, Grandmother. It seems we have little opportunity to see one another. Father sends his greetings and wishes for your good health." Bright Moon spoke graciously, even though she had a very weak connection with the woman.

Bright Moon preferred to consider Black Willow, Matron of the Deer Clan in New Long Pine Village her grandmother on her father's side. After all, she had given birth to him. Goldeneye had adopted her father after he had been taken captive in the raid that had killed her mother's parents.

"Always a pleasure to see you, Granddaughter. Have you brought anything besides traveling clothes? A pretty maiden like you should wear her finest dress in the longhouse of the Head Matron. I would expect that your husband would insist on it," Goldeneye replied in a matronly tone. She looked at Fast Hawk as she finished.

Although they had not been introduced as such, Goldeneye assumed that Bright Moon and Fast Hawk were married. Why else would they travel for several days together?

Goldeneye wore a decorated yellow doeskin dress with clan symbols embroidered in shell beads. Her light-gray hair was wound into a tight bun at the back of her head with goose bone skewers. Her face was a map of wrinkles, obscuring faded tattoos on her chin, cheeks, and temples. She had been a beautiful young woman and carried herself as such, but age had taken its toll on her features. Her lips had shrunk around her mostly toothless jaws, giving her smile a comic appearance. She was a widow now, and attended by two adult daughters, who had been outwardly jealous of their mother's adoption of the boy who should have been no more than a slave. They rejoiced when he married and moved to his wife's village.

"Grandmother, these are the clothes I wear every day. And I am not married. Fast Hawk and I travel together as a convenience. I came to talk to the Head Matron and War Chief about our common enemy, the Haudenosaunee raiders we have had to deal with lately."

"You are an emissary from your mother?" the elder woman pressed.

"I am a warrior here to discuss strategy," Bright Moon replied.

"You are a clan maiden and should act accordingly. Or has your mother not instructed you properly?"

"We have plenty of clan maidens in New Long Pine Village, but too few warriors, Grandmother. That is my role."

"I think it is time to end this feast and let people retire to their longhouses. It will be cold this night," Cool Dawn announced.

When the others left, Cool Dawn, Ten Point, Flat Deer, Fast Hawk, and Bright Moon returned to the firepit with another cup of spruce needle tea.

"Head Matron, War Chief, when Fast Hawk and I were camped on the river four nights past, I scouted upriver before daylight. I discovered a camp of four Haudenosaunee scouts. This is troubling because we have never seen them on the west side of the river before. Have you?" Bright Moon started the conversation.

"No, this is a first. You obviously got around them somehow," Ten Point observed.

"No, we killed them. They were so confident they had no guard watching their camp. We caught them by surprise, killed two and wounded two. We hoped to get some information from those two. Fast Hawk can use their tongue and got some information from one before he died. The other refused to talk. I took the tourniquet from his arm and let him bleed out."

"What did the one tell you?" Cool Dawn asked.

"They are from Ganeco Town. They are following a new leader named Skanatego, who he said is the son of Ganeco. You may remember that Yellow Hair had killed him about ten and nine sun cycles past. This Skanatego believes it is his destiny to rule all the land and all the people from the Ohi-yo River to the Lenape River. That is all we were able to learn. We do not know their numbers or strength, but Ganeco Village is some distance from here. To send warriors this far to fight a war must be very costly," Bright Moon explained.

"They come downriver at times, but their raids are usually carried out by very young warriors in smaller parties. I think we have had some come down from the Roaring Waters, too. We may be dealing with different enemies. Or different coalitions of the same people. My understanding is they are continually fighting each other, making the whole situation unstable and unpredictable," Ten Point offered while noting Cool Dawn deep in thought.

"I will wait until winter has passed, but I wish to come to New Long Pine Village to discuss some options with your leaders. Is that acceptable, warrior maiden?" Cool Dawn directed her question to Bright Moon.

"I am confident you will be most welcome, Head Matron. Our villages need to be united if we are to repel this Haudenosaunee threat."

"You say you have seen only ten and seven sun cycles, but you talk and carry yourself like someone much older," Cool Dawn complimented Bright Moon.

"Thank you, Head Matron. I have had to work harder than the men to gain their respect."

"That is always the case, even though we are supposed to run their lives. Power is a strange partner."

The next day, a public feast was held in honor of the visitors from New Long Pine Village. The day had warmed enough to hold the festivities in the plaza. After the first round of roast venison, dancing started. Bright Moon found herself fending off several warriors trying to impress her. Fast Hawk gained the attention of several young maidens, including White Flower, granddaughter of Cool Dawn.

Bright Moon declared they would leave the following morning. They had been lucky with the weather so far, but that could change any day. They would spend four days and three nights on the river, if the good weather held.

Fast Hawk was in a sour mood when they left Black Bear Village. "Just because you do not enjoy the company of a warrior in your bed is no reason for you to deny me the pleasure of a maiden."

"No one is forcing you to come with me. We can turn around, and I will leave you here. It matters not to me," she replied sharply.

"Not now. I would look stupid and desperate. But how could it have hurt to stay a few more days?"

"This was not a trip to exercise your manhood. We had a two-pronged mission, completed it, and now we must get back before the cold maker invades."

"You take life too serious."

She drove her paddle into the water and worked like a possessed demon to move their craft downriver as fast as she could. They both remained silent until they stopped just as the sun dropped below the western hills.

Nothing beyond required communication occurred the rest of the way back to New Long Pine Village. Each day featured cloudy skies and cold temperatures. All four mornings they awoke to a coating of hard frost. The last morning, they were greeted by a light dusting of snow. Despite the cold temperatures and the closeness of the freezing water, Bright Moon worked up a sweat pushing them downriver as fast as she could.

# CHAPTER 7

# DANCING BUFFALO

Dancing Buffalo was experiencing a bad winter. Their camp had plenty of food —that was not the problem. His three wives took turns coupling with him to keep his heart happy. But his nights were long and sleepless. One thing that bothered him was being chased out of Little Antelope Valley by Bull Heart. *How could a great chief of the real people put up with a sniveling trader of the Shoshone people. On top of that, that eastern snake had humiliated him with her indifference when he took her. No one does that to Dancing Buffalo! And right there in front of his wives, no less. I should have held her captive. By now she would be enjoying my great manhood and would no doubt be carrying my child. Perhaps the next thaw, I will pay a visit to Bull Heart's camp.*

Dancing Buffalo considered his options. The warm winds had been blowing all day, and the snow was rapidly disappearing. By sunset, the open grasslands only showed scattered patches of snow. His warriors would be anxious to hunt the herd of buffalo wintering east of their camp on Lodgepole Creek.

*Surely, Bull Heart's warriors would do the same. I can spare five hunters to accompany me to Bull Heart's camp. With them keeping watch, I will slip into the camp in the middle of the night, snatch the woman, and be gone before anyone could stop me. Her crippled man will be of no help to her against me, even if he is in the lodge.*

Three hands before a sliver of light appeared in the eastern sky, Dancing Buffalo and his party were on the trail to Little Antelope Valley. The snow was nearly gone, but the ground was still frozen and dry. The walking was easy, with few snow drifts in wind shadows that kept the warm winds from eating at the snow. The sky was clear and dry with plenty of starlight to guide them along the familiar trail. Dancing Buffalo's only concern was that the weather would change, bringing a blizzard down on them before they made it back to Lodgepole Creek.

In Bull Heart's camp, most of the warriors, indeed, were north of the Flat River where a large herd of buffalo were wintering. Both Redbone and Sheep Talker accompanied the hunters. They needed to do their part to pay Bull Heart for his generosity. Knowing his camp had nothing to fear from Dancing Buffalo, Bull Heart also went on the hunt. Every man would be needed to haul the meat back from the hunt before the cold maker returned.

Dancing Buffalo and his small party traveled on little food or rest. They followed the Chugwater north for three days before they picked up the faint smell of wood smoke carried on the northwest winds. Before running across any of Bull Heart's scouts, they made an early camp where they could rest. After sunset, the party moved to the ridge overlooking the forks on Antelope Creek. The campfires were clearly visible, and it was easy to spot Bull Heart's large lodge. That is where Dancing Buffalo's target would be found.

They encountered a scout near the crest of the ridge. He was a very young man, and easily subdued. They bound him and put a mink skinball in his mouth. In exchange for his life, he told Dancing Buffalo where the young woman was and how many were in the lodge.

*Only the chief's three wives, the Shoshone girl, two attendants, and the eastern woman. This will be easy.*

When all the camp noises drew to a close for the night, Dancing Buffalo went alone into the camp. He carried scraps of fresh venison to toss to any dogs that were aroused. Slowly, he worked his way to the center of the camp and Bull Heart's big lodge. All was quiet.

Red Petal fell asleep early, but she woke up in a short while with a dream of Dancing Buffalo coming to her. She awoke quietly without disturbing anyone.

But her heart was racing, and she felt her skin crawl. She reached under her blanket and gripped her stiletto in her right hand. She kept her eyes open to acclimate to the dim light of the orange coals in the central firepit.

Shortly, a large figure slipped through the door flap and entered the lodge. Her gut told her who it was. She could not bear to see anyone else get hurt, so she remained still and silent. She forced herself to breathe as if she were sleeping while he determined where she was. Slowly, he made his way from one sleeping woman to the next until he spotted her. A grin turned his serious mouth upward.

Dancing Buffalo felt his manhood rise as he looked down at his victim. He pulled a mink skin ball from his bag, bent down and quickly jammed the furry object into her partially open mouth. Before she could react, he slid one arm under her back, the other under her knees and started to lift.

Suddenly, a searing pain burst from his neck. He pulled his arms back and reached for her arm. Too late, another jab into his bleeding neck. He roared in pain and tried to find her fast moving hands. Blood cascaded from his punctured neck like a mountain stream flush with snow melt. His vision blurred, and he felt dizzy. Suddenly a blow to his back shocked him stiff. He felt the blade slide deep into his chest from the back. He knew he was dead before he collapsed into blackness.

All Red Petal could do was bob her head. The

body of Dancing Buffalo lay heavily across her chest and stomach, pinning her arms at her sides as blood flowed from his wounds.

Meadow Dew thought Red Petal was dead for a heartbeat. When she heard Red Petal straining to cry out, she discovered her friend was quite alive. In the dim light, under the dead chief, Red Petal looked black with all the blood on her.

Meadow Dew ripped the mink ball out of Red Petal's mouth and asked, "Are you well?"

Breathlessly, Red Petal conveyed she was all right, but the heavy warrior was crushing her. By now, Bull Heart's other wives were there to help drag the dead man off the young woman. They had no idea who it was in the darkness, but Red Petal knew the identity before he even entered the lodge.

Warriors and women began to gather outside the lodge to find out what was happening.

"We have had an intruder. He is dead. Get the central fire going so we have light enough to determine who it was."

"It is the evil war chief. He came for me," Red Petal said.

"But he is on Lodgepole Creek with his winter camp. What makes you think it was him?" Sees Across the Valley, Bull Heart's first wife asked.

"Red Petal had a dream that he was coming for her. I woke up. That is why I was ready with my stiletto when he tried to take me away."

Sees Across the Valley looked at the others and shrugged as if to say Red Petal is crazy with emotion.

Two warriors came in and dragged Dancing Buffalo's body out by the now blazing fire.

"It is the chief of the band we chased away from this valley!" someone declared.

Sees Across the Valley looked at Red Petal. "You knew?"

"He has been in my nightmares every time I sleep since he forced himself on me, Head Matron."

"It is over. He cannot hurt you again," Sees Across the Valley said, then looked around at the gathering crowd. There was no hint of a new day in the sky yet. She declared, "Get this filth away from the village. The scalp belongs to Red Petal. Take it, child. It will give you great medicine. The rest of you—return to your lodges and get some sleep."

"Should we hunt for others? Surely this one did not come here alone," Fat Bull, the warrior in charge of the four tens of men who did not go on the hunt asked.

"Send a party of two tens of warriors. Do not engage them if they have large numbers. Capture any you can. We need to learn what this was all about," Bull Heart's wife told the man.

A hand of time before the sun rose, Fat Bull's men found the scout who had been tied and gagged.

"The enemy party was only six warriors. Dancing Buffalo went toward the village alone. They surprised me, bound my arms and legs, and gagged me so I could not yell out. They did not harm me, for some reason. When the chief did not come back, the warriors just sort of faded away and left me tied up as you found me," Running Dog said.

"You have no idea where they went?"

"None. Bound as I was, I never saw them. Their voices just faded away like they were moving, but I could not hear their words. I would guess they were going back along the Chugwater."

"All right. We will stay right here until it gets light, then see if we can follow their tracks. It is hard to believe they would abandon their chief. Of course, it is also hard to believe he would come all this way to take one woman. We will see what we can find in the morning. Get some sleep. I will stay awake to make sure they do not return," Running Dog declared.

Running Dog's party found tracks leading to Chugwater Creek and followed it upstream to the south. The pursuers could tell their quarry was hurrying back to their winter camp. Running Dog called off the chase and returned to Bull Heart's camp and reported what they found to Fat Bull.

Redbone felt a strange urge to get back to Bull Heart's winter camp. He could not explain it, but felt someone was in danger. Bull Heart decided the ten buffalo they had killed so far would burden them enough, so starting back would be a good idea. With travois loaded with buffalo hides, meat, stomachs, and some bones, it would take them at least four days to make it back to the Little Antelope Valley.

As it was, the hunting party arrived just before a major blizzard hit the valley. In no time, snow piled up waist-deep with drifts more than twice that high. Any thought of traveling or hunting was curtailed.

Redbone was appalled, worried, and proud when he saw the enemy chief's scalp hanging on Red Petal's belt. After she told the story, he was more proud than anything. Red Petal was truly remarkable. Still, he was concerned about that dream she related to him. *What spirit stirs in her souls? Can she see things before they happen? How does that work? How can it work?*

––––––––

"I HAD another dream about Red Petal last night," Bright Moon reported to Bright Star.

"Did the evil chief rape her again?" Bright Star asked with Water Mint intently listening.

"No, but he did sneak into the lodge where I think she and Redbone are guests. He was going to try to steal her. In my dream, she heard him coming and waited until he had his arms under her and started to lift when she stabbed him in the neck with a stiletto. She got him stabbed in the neck twice when her friend jammed an obsidian knife into his back. He died and fell on Red Petal, covering her with his blood. It was ghastly. I awoke, and do not know what happened after that."

"Did you see Redbone?"

"No. Somehow, I knew he and many of the other men were off on a hunt to replenish their fresh meat supply. Something about a big thaw in midwinter. I do not know how I know that part."

"I hope this all means they are well and surviving a cold winter." Bright Star said as she lost focus, looking to the past, wishing she could reach out to her sister.

———

THE COLD MAKER stayed in the area of Bull Heart's camp past the spring equinox. Snow was piled deep, and drifts were so high it was impossible to travel from the camp in any direction. Food reserves were running low, and rationing was required. Snowshoes were required for the simple task of foraging for firewood in the nearby forest. Many of the lower, dead branches on the pine trees were buried so deep in snow, it was not possible to get at the dead branches. The sheltered places where wood was plentiful were becoming harder to find.

Then, in the first days of the Awakening Moon, the warm winds blew with a vengeance. If a person could stand or sit in one place for any length of time, he could watch the snow dwindle. Within a few days, bare ground was visible everywhere except the wind shadows of large rocks or cliffs. Little of it was melting so the streams received little runoff from the rapidly shrinking snowbanks.

The winds were so strong, it was difficult to stand in open areas. Broken branches were continually blowing into the village, replenishing the firewood supply. But it was not safe to have a fire lit anyway. The winds would carry any live coals into the grasslands where uncontrollable grass fires would sweep across the plains, consuming anything in their path. It was a continuous task, day and night to keep even the lowest lodges from sailing away. Finally, after ten and two days, the winds subsided, and more permanent repairs could be made.

Redbone and Red Petal pitched in and helped where they could. In a quiet time, Redbone approached Sheep Talker.

"Should we be making preparations to move to your people's village?" Redbone asked his guide.

Sheep Talker laughed. "Does Redbone think the cold maker has gone for the summer? She is only gathering her strength for another storm. No, we should remain here at least four, maybe five, tens of days. Even then, she may have a surprise or two in store for weary travelers. Remember, the animals have been dealing with the cold and snow, too. The elk and deer will not be fat for moons. We need to give them a chance to put on some new flesh before we can expect to get much nourishment from them."

"So, this is truly the Starving Moon, even though we thought that was behind us."

"You see my point! Another thing. In just a couple of tens of days, the big bears will be coming out of hibernation. They will be hunting anything that moves until they replace the flesh they lost in the cold times. It is good to stay away from the places they might be...which could be almost anywhere."

"I am not interested in testing myself against one of those anytime soon."

"The mothers with cubs are the real deadly bears. If they see you as a threat, they will come after you. Do anything you can to not get between a mother bear and her cubs. Sometimes it is unavoidable. Those little bears are curious and wander everywhere. Whatever you do, do not make a move toward a cub, if you happen to see one."

"Who would guess the females are the dangerous ones?"

"I can see that!" Red Petal jumped into the conversation. "All mothers put their little ones' safety before their own. It is a natural thing."

"You have a wise wife, my friend," Sheep Talker said.

## CHAPTER 8
# SPRING

"You have seen ten and eight sun cycles now. You are considered the best archer and the most accomplished warrior in the village. Do you not think it is time you found out what those powerful thighs of yours could do with a man in their grip?" Elkhorn asked. He had seen ten and eight sun cycles himself. His family moved to the Deer Clan in New Long Pine Village over two sun cycles past. Elkhorn was handsome, strong, and a very accomplished warrior. He wanted to prove he was a better warrior than Bright Moon, and he intended to have her in his blankets.

"Not interested." Was her curt reply.

They were scouting for evidence of Haudenosaunee activity east and north of the village.

"Come on, now. We are already a good distance from any of our other scouts. We could take a roll and be done before anyone knew. You can keep up your precious reputation and still have some fun."

"Not interested," Bright Moon repeated. Her sharp gaze caught a movement many tens of paces away.

"You are a fool, thinking you can get through life without coupling. Even your fabled aunt found a man."

"My 'fabled aunt' was chosen by power. She did what power desired, and they rewarded her with a one-of-a-kind man, made especially for her."

"Maybe that is why I have come into your life. Have you thought of that? I am the only one who can match you with a bow, and I am confident I can beat you in wrestling or any contest that requires strength."

"Will you shut up? We have five warriors headed this way, and they are not friends of ours."

"Where? I see nothing." He looked in the direction she was concentrating. At last, he thought he saw movement through the trees a great distance to the east. "You cannot pick out any details on them. They are probably hunters from Black Bear Village."

"They are Haudenosaunee scouts. I have seen them many times. We will stay here and keep an eye on them. If they get too close, we will kill a couple of them. I would like to capture one so we can question him."

"How? We cannot speak their animal tongue and

there are too many for us to kill four and capture one. We should go find the others for help."

"You are free to go. I see enemies before me, and I will not let them near my village. If I can capture one, Fast Hawk can speak their tongue some. He could get information about their plans."

"So, you are just going to grab one? What if they shoot back. Are you willing to die for a little information that will probably be all lies?"

"My intention would be that they are the ones doing the dying."

"You are crazy. You think they will just let you shoot arrows at them, without shooting back? That is a stupid plan. I bet the war chief would disapprove."

"You can watch if you want. Just do not get in my way when shit starts happening."

A hand of time later, the Haudenosaunee scouts were strung out, the closest about ten bow shots distant. They were moving slowly on a game trail that ran east and west. Bright Moon had hunted along that trail extensively.

She lowered her voice to a whisper. "I will wait until the second man is in bow range. I will kill him first, then the first one. After that, it will depend on what the others do."

"You are insane! But maybe I could sneak over to that hill to the left and drop the next one in line."

"Too late. You move now, and they will see you. Wait until I shoot and see what they do."

"Who do you think you are? Just because your father is War Chief does not mean I am compelled to do as you say."

"I think if you try to sneak over there, you will blow our cover, and we will not accomplish a thing. Are you going to fight with me, or against me?"

"Well, I want to be against you, so I will fight with you." He looked at her chest with a predator's smile on his face.

She ignored him and concentrated on the warriors as they approached. Only three had their bows strung and none had pulled an arrow from their quivers. The first was now within her bow's range. She waited. She had five arrows laying on the ground in front of her.

As the second man in their loose line move into her range, she drew her bow back and released. The arrow penetrated deep into the warrior's chest with a thud. The first man in line had his arrow nocked and was looking for his target when he heard the hiss of her second arrow just before it drove into his chest. The arrow went between two ribs, clipped a lung, passed through his beating heart, and slammed into a back rib. By then, his shocked heart had quit beating. Both men were dead.

The third man turned to run out of bow range. He did not make it as her next arrow smashed into his back with enough force to break a rib, pass through a lung, and come to a rest against his sternum. He fell on his face, trying to get enough air into his lungs to stay alive.

The other two turned to flee as fast as their feet would carry them. Bright Moon was faster. Before they had gone two tens of tens of paces, she was right on their heels. She shouted the Haudenosaunee word that Fast Hawk had taught her meant "Stop!" One man stopped, the other ran on, but his escape ended when another of her arrows pierced his back, knocking him to the ground.

The one who had stopped saw an opportunity when she fired that last arrow. He pulled a war club and stalked after her. She already planned for that and had her cub drawn and ready to fight. He aggressively came after her, swinging his club in an arc that she could not penetrate. She feinted a swing, then backed off when his swing arced down to block her thrust. His club only swung through empty air. But when his club reached belt level on its way downward, her club followed his arm. When he reached the end of his swing, her club struck his arm with enough force to break his ulna.

He whimpered, knowing her next swing would crush his skull. That swing never came. Instead, she stood before him with the fury of a female bear separated from her cubs.

"Warrior talk?" Bright Moon asked the man, who, she guessed, had seen less than two tens and five sun cycles.

Quivering, he held out his broken arm and asked, "Healer? Diving Loon will live?"

"Healer" and "live" were the only words she understood, but she nodded.

"Diving Loon talk." She heard talk, and she nodded more vigorously.

Suddenly Elkhorn was at her side. "Where have you been?" she asked.

"The others are all dead. What will you do with him?" He had his war club in hand and thumped it into her prisoner's ribs.

"Do not hurt him. We are taking him back for questioning. I promised we will fix his arm if he talks."

"You get dumber every minute. Anything he says will be a lie. We should just kill him now."

She noted the blood and brain matter on the ball of his club. "What were you doing when I was killing those others?"

"You told me to watch, so I watched."

"And then you went behind me and clubbed them to make sure they were dead?"

"What else would I do? They are enemies and deserve no mercy from us."

"True. But I do not know. Maybe you could have joined the fight. You know, make sure none could have gotten to me, like this one did." She pointed to the warrior who had sat down and cradled his broken arm.

"I thought you wanted him alive."

"Never mind. I do not care about these others, but I need to get this wounded man to a healer. You have not earned them, but you can have any weapons you want. If you find a map of any kind, make sure Red Hand gets it."

The wounded warrior needed several rests and water breaks before Bright Moon brought him into New Long Pine Village three hands of time later.

Later, with splint on his set broken arm, Bright Moon had Fast Hawk talk to him. She learned his name is Diving Loon, and he belongs to the Duck Clan in Ganeco Town. She fed the questions and listened carefully to the translated answers. She thought Fast Hawk did not have a real firm grasp of the Haudenosaunee tongue. The questions seemed to confuse the warrior, and his answers were ambiguous, at best.

She did find out that Skanatego was their war chief and political chief as well. All the warriors and all the men and women answered to him. Supposedly he is a cunning war leader and the number of warriors at his disposal is practically unlimited. Many refugees are fleeing south from wars between bands of Haudenosaunee villages. With the Lenape people giving up the western branch of the Mud River, Skanatego controlled a vast area with a few small communities and scattered homesteads.

The New Long Pine Village Council of Elders voted, by a narrow margin, to stake the man to a post in the plaza and let the spouses of warriors slain by

Haudenosaunee raiders do whatever they wished to him. Some on the Council recalled the horrendous actions of the Black Bear warriors so many sun cycles past and felt sentencing this warrior in some way avenged the suffering of that attack. He would be given a mouthful of water each day, but no food. The warrior would live as long as those spouses let him. The small cuts and burns, in addition to the mutilation of his genitals weakened him rapidly. He lasted only a day and a half.

After he died, Bright Star called the Council together and thoroughly reprimanded them for voting to do the thing they swore would never happen in New Long Pine Village. "How short your memories are! Every elder in this room who was there said, 'Never again' with bitter tears in your eyes. Then, you turn around and sentence that young man, who was probably only guilty of being a poor warrior, to the same treatment. I, as Head Matron of this village, hang my head in shame at your actions!"

Someone hiding in the crowd of spectators called out, "What would you do, Head Matron? Turn him loose to come back and fight against us? Let him bring strategic information to his war leaders? He had to die here!"

"You are right, Stone Hawk of the Hawk Clan, he did need to die. But a swift death by a war club to the skull would have been preferable to the torture inflicted upon him by us. When word of this day gets out, I hope our village is not shunned by the rest of the Monongahela Nation. I have spoken." Bright Star stepped away from the front of the room.

"Very well said." Water Mint hugged her niece.

"Bright Moon, you brought that prisoner in. What did you want to see done to him?" Bright Star asked her daughter.

"I wanted to feed him full of false information and send him home after he healed. I thought he was better as a tool than a victim of some hideous revenge," Bright Moon answered honestly.

"You are as wise as your father gives you credit for," Water Mint told Bright Moon.

## CHAPTER 9
# VISITORS

The Ohi-yo was back to a more normal flow after the spring floods. Bright Moon watched the four Black Bear Canoes slide onto the New Long Pine Village canoe landing. She noted Cool Dawn, Ten Point, Flat Deer, and a surprise, the maiden White Flower, daughter of Light of Dawn, daughter of Cool Dawn. *Looks like Fast Hawk will be happy. But I do not see a match for Elkhorn in any of those canoes.*

"Greetings, Black Bear Village, welcome to New Long Pine Village," Bright Moon announced.

"Good to see you alive and well, daughter of Bright Star," Cool Dawn responded.

The formal introductions were conducted by Bright Star for New Long Pine Village and Cool Dawn for Black Bear Village. Bright Moon noted that Fast Hawk and White Flower had found each other and were sitting together in one of the outer rows of onlookers.

Cool Dawn requested a private meeting with Bright Star, Red Hand, and Bright Moon before she addressed the Council of Elders. Permission was granted.

Cool Dawn and Ten Point sat to Bright Star's right side. Red Hand and Bright Moon sat to Bright Star's left side. Bright Star's seat was covered with a mountain lion hide while the others sat on tanned deer hides.

"You requested this meeting, Cool Dawn. You may have the floor," said Bright Star.

"Thank you, Bright Star. I will start by saying that the surprise visit by Bright Moon to Black Bear Village last autumn was very productive. She has a very mature mind for one so young. Her words, in fact, inspired me to develop a plan that I think both our villages will find beneficial." She let that soak in for a moment.

"Beneficial for both villages always sounds good," Bright Star quipped.

"My proposal is based on the aggressive nature of our mutual enemy, the Haudenosaunee. I know there are of many bands of Haudenosaunee to our north. Some of those bands form nations and alliances now and again, but their nature is to be aggressive and fight among themselves as well as with outsiders, like us." She used her fingers to indicate the commonality between Black Bear and New Long Pine Villages. Bright Star and Red Hand nodded in unison.

"But in reality, Black Bear and New Long Pine would not be able to provide any mutual aid with our villages so far apart. My proposal is that we should be significantly closer. Close enough that a call to aid could be executed quickly and efficiently." Heads nodded all around.

"We have not picked out an exact location yet, but the Black Bear Village Council of Elders has authorized me to negotiate a suitable site for a new Black Bear Village."

Momentarily stunned, memories of Black Bear Village turning evil and invading Long Pine Village, changing her life forever, brought tears to Bright Star's eyes.

Noting Bright Star's reaction, Cool Dawn looked at her and softly said, "Yes, that was a bad time for all of us. But I think, I hope, we are past all that now. This village has been here for nearly two tens of sun cycles. I think we can live together in peace, now."

"Yes, of course we have moved well beyond those dark days. I would be delighted to have a neighbor village to share ideas and common defense with." Bright Star seemed to get past her fears as she talked.

"A hand of time upriver there is an excellent village location. I think Bright Star's sister chose this site over that one simply because this one is closer to the old Long Pine Village site." Red Hand offered as he looked around for responses, settling his eyes on his daughter.

"I am all in favor of doubling our warrior force and will support the effort any way I can," Bright Moon added.

"Perhaps tomorrow, we could go look at a couple of these proposed sites, then meet with your Council tomorrow evening?" Cool Dawn inquired.

"If we get an early start. I will announce to the Council what we are up to. You all can get to your sleeping robes," Bright Star replied.

At the official Council meeting the following evening, Cool Dawn announced that with New Long Pine cooperation, the Black Bear warriors and women could have fields cleared, planted, and frames built for longhouses built before harvest. In the spirit of cooperation and better defenses against marauding Haudenosaunee, the New Long Pine Council of Elders declared full support and cooperation. New Long Pine warriors would provide meat for the Black Bear villagers working on building the new community.

Bright Moon never laid eyes on a single enemy scout all spring and right up to the Green Corn Celebration. Still, she felt they were being watched the whole summer. She stayed, along with four tens of New Long Pine warriors to guard the village and the new village site while many others attended the Summer Solstice Celebration at Monongahela Village. The highlight of which was the funeral of the Beloved Trader who had been married to the Beloved Head Matron before she passed.

While her family was gone, Bright Moon experienced more vivid dreams about Redbone and Red Petal. They were spending the summer high in the mountains with their *Newe* (Shoshone) friends. They were accumulating trade goods but were not sure when they would leave Tall Ram's village. The summer camp was high where they ate many animals that wore curled horns on their heads, especially large, thick horns on the big males. In her dreams, she had also seen a strange animal that looked like a small deer but had odd-shaped black horns on their heads and a lot of white on their bodies. Those animals ran very fast and could see very well in the open grasslands. There were some elk and buffalo as well.

In one dream, Redbone was hunting with some warriors, and a giant bear came after them. All of the warriors shot arrows into the beast as fast as they could. The bear became confused, apparently not knowing which man was causing it the most pain. When Redbone fired his fifth arrow into the big bear's chest, it staggered and fell. All totaled there were more than two tens of arrows sticking out of the huge animal. That happened before they arrived at the high camp at the edge of the tree line. During the Solstice Celebration high in their mountain camp, Red Petal told Redbone she was with child.

They would stay with Tall Ram's people at least another sun cycle.

*These dreams seem too real to me. I think, somehow, I am looking into their lives. I wish I knew more about controlling the dreams. As far as I know, they just come to me randomly. I wonder if I should try to find them. From what I have heard, it could take many sun cycles to track down someone in those vast lands. Face it. I can go nowhere as long as this Haudenosaunee problem is hanging over us.*

———

BY THE END of the corn harvest and the Green Corn Celebration, the Black Bear villagers had eight long-house frames built with three partially covered with bark slabs. They should all be ready to live in before snow flies. Bright Moon spent much of her time scouting for enemy movements in the forests east of the now dual villages.

One day in the Hunter's Moon, while she was scouting to the north of where warriors were collecting large slabs of bark to cover the new lodges, she picked up the scent of burning wood on the northeast breeze. She slipped off in the direction the wind was coming from. The further north she got, the stronger the smell.

All day long, she followed that scent. *My inkling is that the enemy is burning the abandoned Black Bear Village. I better get back and report this to Father.*

It was well into the night when she finally slid past the door hanging at the east entrance of the Water Plant Clan longhouse. No one was awake, so she went straight to her bed chamber. Her mind was full of scenarios that could play out in the war with their Haudenosaunee enemies. But her body was so exhausted, she was asleep in a few heartbeats.

She was awoken by the scent of corn mush and sassafras tea wafting through the longhouse. She hurried out to take care of her personal business, then joined Water Mint, Tallow, her mother, and father at the firepit.

"You must have come in quite late last night," said Bright Star.

"I did. Father, yesterday I was scouting northeast of where the warriors are harvesting bark slabs for the new longhouses. I picked up a faint odor of burning wood riding on that north wind. As I tracked into the wind, the scent got stronger. When I realized how late it was, I made it back here as quickly as I could."

"What did you think it was, a large enemy camp?" Red Hand asked.

"I did not know, and I still do not. But I am guessing it is Haudenosaunee burning the abandoned village. It would not surprise me to see them build a new village there, kind of like a wolf pack marks a new territory when they move in."

"Did you have anything in mind you wish to do about it?"

"Nothing specific, but can we afford for them to move in so close to us?"

"Good question for the council," Bright Star added.

"Should I pack some food and scout all the way to the old village to see with my own eyes what is going on there?"

"Take someone with you. I do not want you doing that alone." Bright Star left no room for debate.

"It will take longer, and I will be forced to fight off some young man's advances." Bright Moon could not refrain from registering a complaint.

Bright Star started to reply, but Red Hand cut her off. "Take Fast Hawk. He knows the way, and he will want to get back to White Flower's company quickly."

As different scenarios played out in her mind, Bright Moon decided to take a few extra things. In the storage section of the longhouse, she found a coil of strong cord, several hand-lengths long. The crafty woman noted some jars filled with pine oil. She stuck two in her pack, along with two stone hand axes.

# CHAPTER 10
# DELAYING THE ENEMY

F our days later, Bright Moon and Fast Hawk hid their canoe in some brush along a small creek on the east bank of the Ohi-yo about a day's hike downstream of the abandoned Black Bear Village site. The scent of wood smoke was clearly evident in the northern breeze. The day was overcast, but rain did not feel imminent.

They climbed to a high ridge from which they would be able to see the village site and still be a good distance away. As expected, the burned palisade resembled a wolf's jaw with poles burned unevenly along the perimeter of the village. All of the longhouses lay in heaps, most smoldering. The villagers had left nothing of value, so a handful of warriors were making sure everything in them burned to a pile of ashes.

In an abandoned crop field close by, there were four piles of freshly cut and stripped saplings that would be used in the construction of new longhouses.

"It would be a shame if those new poles accidentally caught afire and were rendered useless for construction, would it not?" Bright Moon whispered the question to Fast Hawk.

"You want to sneak down there, set fire to a bunch of green poles, and slip away without arousing six warriors armed with bows, axes, and clubs? Plus, however many scouts they have in the surrounding area watching for people like us. You are crazier than a fox trapped between a forest fire and a lake!"

"You are not a very brave individual, are you? Of course, we wait until nightfall. Those piles of poles are a good distance from any of the fires. We slip down there long after sunset, when everyone is snug in their sleeping robes. We carefully and quietly carry some very dry kindling to the side of each pile of poles. When all is ready, we set each pile of kindling afire, then slip off into the darkness, work our way back up here, and enjoy the show. When they are all involved trying to put out those poles, we will be hustling back to our canoe and fleeing downriver."

"And if anything goes wrong, which it always does, we will be killed or captured, which I suspect will be worse for you than me."

"Then we better make sure nothing goes wrong. Let us work our way down to the edge of that field. If this cloudy sky prevails, it will be black as pitch when the sun goes down."

"Yes, so how do you propose finding our way back up this wooded slope in that darkness?"

"That is why we go now, so we can learn the way. Memorize it!"

"You are so smart, maybe I should just stay here and let you go by yourself."

"You could, but I wonder how White Flower would feel about that?"

"Of course you would use that against me!"

"I am trying to hurt our enemy here, and all you want to do is complain. If you are not going to take it seriously, just head back to the canoe now. I am better off by myself than with a reluctant partner!"

"And you sure know how to cut deep."

"Like I said once before, war is cold. You coming or not?"

"I am coming."

"Good. Gather the driest pine and spruce branches you can find on the way down. Go slow, stay quiet, and study the trail. No more talking until we know we are away from them."

She worked her way down the hill. Most of it was a well-used game trail, probably enhanced by Black Bear warriors through many seasons. Once at the bottom, they were well screened by brush bordering the field.

She pulled two stoppered ceramic jars from her pack and handed one to him.

"What is this?" he whispered.

"Just in case, I brought a little accelerant. I was concerned our firewood might get wet, so I threw in some pine oil. Drizzle some of that on a few of your poles and your pile of kindling, and our fires will burn faster and hotter. They will not have time to chase us."

Fast Hawk just shook his head. *She is just a girl. How does she come up with these ideas?*

They did not have to wait long before the light grew dimmer. The three pairs of warriors left heaps of what had been longhouses burning as they made their way to the east across an open field to a stand of hemlock trees. The heavily needled limbs and branched screened the warriors' campsite from Bright Moon and Fast Hawk's position. He looked at her, and she smiled. In no time, it was very dark, but the enemy warriors had a campfire going in those trees that flickered through the screen now and then. Soon enough the fire burned down, and a dull orange glow wavered every now and then.

After a while, no more activity or noises could be detected from the warrior campsite. Bright Moon looked up, and no starlight penetrated the cloud cover. It was essentially dark as charcoal.

Bright Moon rose to her feet and picked up her bundle of kindling, which was now bound in a loop of cord. She carefully pulled the cord until the bundle was almost to her shoulders. She hoped her partner had listened to her. She had directed him to the closest two bundles of poles while she went to the more distant ones. It was so dark she could not tell where the bundles were until she was right at them.

She indicated to him to unload one bundle of kindling at that pile, then follow her. She had him ready to strike his spark stones when she had her first fire lit. With Fast Hawk ready, she moved on to the two piles she planned to burn.

Just as she left the end of the second pile of poles, she heard a man grunt like he had been sitting and stood up. He could not have been twenty paces from her. *He must be guarding these poles. I will have to get rid of him before I can proceed.*

*What can I do? Walk silently up to him and plant your knife in his heart. Yes, nothing to it!* she mocked herself. She set the bundle of kindling silently on the dark ground and started into the space between the piles of poles where she had heard the man stand up. Slowly she crossed the space. She thanked the creator for the bed of short weeds, softened by a recent rain, that were just beginning to die in the abandoned field, cushioning her slow, careful steps.

Less than two paces from her quarry, she heard him take a breath. *He has heard me. He was holding his breath, listening.* She gripped her knife and cocked her arm for a strike. The guard nervously sucked in a breath. She used that as a guide and struck for his throat as fast and hard as she could. She felt the knife penetrate the soft skin of his neck. He stiffened as her body struck his, but they barely moved before hitting the pile of poles he was standing next to.

A flood of hot liquid flowed down her arm as the man's body went limp. Then she realized she was holding a dead man up against the pole pile. His loosened bowels told her that her attack was successful. She struggled lowering his limp body to the ground.

Hurrying, she retrieved her bundle of kindling, rushed to the next pile, almost crashing into it. Setting half of her kindling next to the pile, she dribbled some pine oil, retrieved her striking stones and produced a spark that caught in the kindling. Quickly as she could manage, she returned to her other pole pile, dowsed the kindling and the warrior's shirt, and struck her stone. Instantly flames spread to the drops of pine oil. She never looked back.

Shouts broke out over at the warriors' camp just as she called for Fast Hawk.

"Over here," she heard him hiss. *Good, he was smart enough to move away from the growing light of the burning poles.*

She grabbed his arm and pulled. "Let us get away from here." With her leading, they sprinted for the brush at the base of the hill. Nearly crashing into the brush, somehow, she found the trail they had come down and started up it. Fast Hawk right at her heels, she scampered up the steep hill practically on all fours. Her muscles burned, and her breath came hard, but she never slowed.

Finally, the ground leveled as they reached the top of the ridge. Looking back for the first time, she saw four large fires burning out of control. In the glow, she saw five figures standing back from the flame. They just stood there as if they had nothing else to do. Bright Moon and Fast Hawk looked on from the ridge for nearly a finger of time while they recovered their breathing.

Finally, she grabbed his arm and said, "We better get out of here. As soon as it is light enough, they will be following our tracks."

"I need, we both need, rest!" Fast Hawk argued.

"We can rest after we get in the canoe. We can just float downriver. Right now, we need to get away from here." She dragged him down the trail toward the river. By the time they got on the river, the sky was just losing its black color.

"You rest. I am still full of energy from what we pulled off back there. I will keep us in deep water. You can sleep," Bright Moon offered.

The sky was getting light fast, even though it was still overcast with gray clouds. He looked back at her. And saw her arm and chest were covered with drying blood. "What happened? Are you hurt?"

"No, not at all. It seems they had a guard posted around those pole piles. By some magic, I detected him first. I was able get my knife out and jammed it into his neck before he could react. My momentum carried us into the side of that stack of poles. I was holding him against the pile when I realized he was dead."

"You are a cold one."

"Remember that!"

"You need not worry. I have White Flower to keep me warm now."

"Light of Dawn approves?"

"Yes."

"Congratulations. When is the wedding?"

"I do not know. After the village is finished, I suppose.

"I think our mission may have brought the war closer to a conclusion. This Skanatego will either bring an all-out attack or back off completely. Now his whole summer of cutting, trimming, and aging longhouse poles has been wasted. If I have him figured out, I think he will lead every warrior he has against us. It will be our chance to get him and put this thing to rest."

"Or it could be the end of us."

"There is that."

"That is a dangerous game you are playing. Is it worth the gamble?"

"Better to gamble that he will leave us alone? He has already said he plans to own us all. I am not in favor of that."

"I have heard it said that it is better to be a live slave than a dead warrior for a lost cause."

"I am afraid I must disagree with whoever said that."

"So, you are willing to wager that most feel as you do?"

"Most do not even know the wolf is at the door until it is torn from the lodge. If I can, I will not let the wolf get that close."

"Interesting."

Four days later when then New Long Pine canoe landing came into sight, Bright Moon said, "Fast Hawk, you performed well on this mission. I confess that you showed more bravery than I gave you credit for. You should be proud of how you conducted yourself."

*Great, just when I was going to her mother and father to tell them what a cold-hearted bitch they had raised. Now I must remain the humble warrior willing to do whatever she wishes.*

"Thank you," Fast Hawk replied tentatively.

"What did you find" Red Hand asked after she poured herself a cup of tea and sat in her place at the firepit.

She told them what she and Fast Hawk had found, and the action they took.

"That sounds like a decision for the Council, my rebellious daughter," said Bright Star.

"Mother, you know that by the time we came back to the village, we would have lost any opportunity to slow them down some. I suspect they were just going to build on that site as a way of rubbing salt in our wounds. Now they have salt in their wounds."

Bright Star looked to Red Hand for support.

"Bright Moon, you are putting a lot of faith in what a scout told Fast Hawk. We are confident that he does not understand the Haudenosaunee tongue as well as he thinks he does. Given that, and we all know scouts are told to say all kinds of things to keep from being tortured or killed. Did you take these things into account? You may have escalated this war out of control when it was not necessary." Red Hand now looked to Bright Star for approval of his words. She nodded.

"To start with, that scout up on the river was dying with an arrow in his gut. He was beyond lying, and it was too late for mercy. Besides that, the frequent attempted raids tell me this Skanatego absolutely plans to conquer us. Now that we are consolidated with Black Bear, I think Skanatego can be lured into action and defeated. Cut the head off the snake, so to speak."

"You have thought a lot about this," Bright Star said.

"Yes."

"You are young, but perhaps your words carry more truth than we give you credit for. We are probably safe now until spring. Maybe we can have a plan by then. Thank you for your insight and determination, my daughter." Bright Star stared straight ahead, seeing deeply into the past.

# CHAPTER II

# FRUSTRATION

"Red Bear, what are you doing here? You are supposed to be preparing the old Black Bear Village for the Real People to move onto that site. It is part of my plan to occupy the Ohi-yo River Valley." Skanatego was beside himself with anger at his deputy war chief returning long before he should have.

Red Bear cringed before confessing, "Chief Skanatego, there has been a major setback. Someone burned all of the poles we had stockpiled to erect four new longhouses."

"What? How could that happen? You had guards?"

"Yes, my chief. We had only one more day of burning the last of those squat little piles of trash they call lodges. That night, my brother was on guard duty. We found his body badly burned next to one of the pole piles. It was hard to tell, but I think his throat was slit."

"So, you are telling me I was ill-advised to send you to do a simple job."

"They came in the middle of the night. Our entire crew was exhausted from the previous ten days of burning the palisade, longhouses, and any other trace of those worm-rotted Monongahela snakes. The rest of us slept while my brother kept watch. His tracks indicated he walked around and between the pole piles as he was ordered. We found no place where he stopped to sleep."

"This is unbelievable. Do you have any more excuses, or can I order you thrashed within a breath of your cowardly life with a willow branch now?"

"There is more, my chief. There were just two sets of tracks. One, a normal sized man, the other, a woman, judging by the size of the tracks. They looked like the same pattern as the ones we found around where that scout party was ambushed over by New Long Pine Village."

"You are saying some woman is wreaking havoc on my plans? Who is this woman?"

"I know not, my chief. It could be a small man, I suppose. But the tracks are a bit shorter and narrower than most man tracks."

"Where did she go? Please do not tell me you did not pursue these marauders."

"They came across the abandoned field just

south of the village. Then fled back across that same field. We followed their tracks over the ridge to the next valley. They followed a small creek that flows into the river. They had a canoe under some brush and started downriver. We could not find the tracks until the next morning, but they must have fled during the night. By the time we could have gone back to our camp, loaded gear and supplies, we could never have caught them before they returned to New Long Pine Village. We came straight here to report what happened."

"And now we have no time to organize an attack before the cold maker arrives. It appears I must find a way to get this snake troublemaker away from her village and have a little talk with her. Let me think about that. Now, get out of my sight before I have you tortured for your incompetence."

Skanatego spent many sleepless nights trying to decide on a strategy for eliminating the woman warrior who seemed to be leading the Monongahela people against his forces. At last, a plan formed. Mink is the perfect instrument for this plan to succeed. That night, in their sleeping skins, he gave his daughter her orders to find, seduce, and capture or kill this woman messing with his plan.

———

EARLY IN THE Moon of the Winter Solstice, Bright Moon was scouting and hunting deer east of her village. Since she and Fast Hawk successfully delayed Skanatego from rebuilding Black Bear Village, every hunt was a scouting mission. This day she brought Elkhorn, Fast Hawk, and Gray Dove, a woman warrior who was one of the best archers in New Long Pine Village. Bright Moon had taken her under her wing and taught her how to strengthen her upper body to be able to use a stronger bow, capable of extra-long shots from the palisade wall.

They set up just a short distance into the slash line protecting the palisade from a large-scale attack. Several large trees had been felled and left, providing good cover while being able to see out into the thinner surrounding forest to the east of New Long Pine Village.

The same group had set up in the same places for five days running, without seeing any enemy. Gray Dove and Elkhorn had managed to bring down a couple deer that wandered too close.

On the sixth day, an enemy scout made an appearance. But something was off. Bright Moon noted that the hooded scout would move only about two or three tens of paces, stop, and look to certain locations behind him. She tried to see what he was seeing. Finally, she watched a bush move some five tens of paces behind him. Then she focused on the next place the scout seemed to be watching, and saw another bush move.

*I see! Guards are following the scout. I expect they are waiting for the scout to take an arrow, then rush in and capture whoever shot the arrow at the scout. Clever. Too bad it will not work, at least not this time.* A bluejay scolding call, repeated four times, told her companions there were four enemies, not one strange scout.

Gray Dove was close enough that Bright Moon could mouth words to her. Gray Dove should wound the scout with an arrow to his calf. Bright Moon would take out the next warrior who would be using the bush disguise. Hopefully, Fast Hawk and Elkhorn will get the other two. Using hand signals, Bright Moon told Fast Hawk to her left, and Elkhorn to her right, how they would handle the fight. It was imperative to her to capture one of them.

Bright Moon and Gray Dove drew back their bows. Gray Dove's target was obvious, Bright Moon's would be a guess as to what part of that bush the enemy was hidden in. Gray Dove let her arrow fly first. It stuck in the scout's calf muscle causing a painful scream. More of a high-pitched scream than Bright Moon had expected.

The bush moved enough to give Bright Moon a target, and her arrow swiftly eliminated that warrior. Seeing where her arrow came from, the two remaining warriors shucked their bush hides and bows, let out screaming war cries, and charged Bright Moon's position with raised war clubs. They never saw the projectiles coming at them from the sides. Both died quickly with arrows through their chests.

Bright Moon and Gray Dove slowly approached

the wounded scout. To their surprise, the warrior's hood fell away, revealing a woman. Bright Moon was instantly glad Gray Dove shot true and only wounded the young woman, who she guessed had not seen two tens of sun cycles yet.

Using pigeon and sign, Bright Moon told the woman her leg would be treated. The young woman replied in kind, "Fix leg, men use White Fox?"

Bright Moon shook her head vigorously, "No! No one use White Fox. I am Bright Moon, Second War Chief, New Long Pine Village. Give word no one hurt White Fox. Bright Moon need White Fox teach tongue."

White Fox started to reach for her stiletto. Bright Moon dropped and restrained her hand before White Fox had cleared her stiletto from its place in her belt.

"Bright Moon plan to stop war between our peoples."

"Bright Moon foolish. Skanatego no stop war until he control Ohi-yo Valley."

"He lose more people than us."

"He has more people to lose. He no care."

"We help White Fox to healer, fix leg. Teach Bright Moon tongue."

"Maybe."

Both women saw more in each other's eyes than they bargained for.

Fast Hawk and Elkhorn had taken the weapons from the dead and came to where Bright Moon and

Gray Dove were just finished putting a bandage on the wounded scout.

Elkhorn looked at White Fox and said, "Want me to take care of her? I can make her talk." He looked at the captive with his sweetest smile.

"No, you and everyone else will leave her alone. She will teach me the Haudenosaunee tongue, then we will decide what to do with her. Right now, you can carry weapons while Gray Dove and I help her to the village." Bright Moon left no room for argument.

"Oh, will she be sleeping in your chamber? Otherwise, you never know what some handsome warrior might have in mind." Elkhorn gave Bright Moon a lascivious grin.

"Keep pushing, and you might find yourself in more pain than you can handle," Bright Moon replied humorlessly.

Bright Moon and Gray Dove put White Fox's arms over their shoulders and started for their village.

Fast Hawk looked at Elkhorn. "You know, she is very serious and very capable of hurting you. You best keep that in mind."

As Bright Moon and Gray Dove made their way to the village, Gray Dove said, "I wish I had the words to put warriors in their place like you do. More often than not, I end up sharing blankets with them because I do not want to offend them. But you just shut them right off. I admire you for that."

"You just have to decide for yourself whether or

not you want what they offer. I have never wanted that, so it is easy for me to say 'No.' The words I use depend on the circumstances. Elkhorn has been pushing me for some time now, and I have about run out of patience with him. One of these days he is going to feel the ball of my war club slam into his manhood. I do not think he will find that so funny. Just remember, if you make a threat, you must follow through with it. If you do not, you will never be rid of them."

"I will try."

"No, you cannot 'try,' you must 'do,' and expect nothing less from yourself. Understand?"

"I do, and I will!" *But for some reason, I am not sure I can say no to Elkhorn.*

White Fox could not understand the words but picked up on what the other women were saying. All the way from Ganeco Town, she had moved from one warrior to another. She had to keep them eating out of her hand. Now, they were all dead.

Bright Moon and Gray Dove stopped at Willow Bark's lodge and the healer checked White Fox's wound. She cleaned the site where the arrow passed through her calf without striking any bones. Willow Bark sewed up the entry and exit wounds and applied a poultice while she had White Fox drink some special tea. Finally, she put a splint on the leg to keep it immobile while the shin healed.

Gray Dove returned to the Hawk Clan longhouse, collected her weapons from Fast Hawk, and sent

Elkhorn away. He had been waiting with Fast Hawk, planning to spend the night in Gray Dove's sleeping skins. Instead, she sent him away emphatically. She was too tired to deal with any man. Fast Hawk was occupied with White Flower, so he was not a problem.

# CHAPTER 12

# WHITE FOX

B right Moon and White Fox sat at the Water Plant Clan firepit relating the story of their day while they ate turkey stew. Bright Moon told Bright Star her plans to keep White Fox with her until she learned the Haudenosaunee tongue.

"You trust this enemy warrior enough to let her stay in your chamber?" Red Hand asked.

"Yes, I do. She has related to me that Skanatego is a fool. She signed to me that if he is eliminated, the war will end."

"Why do they not vote him out of his position?" Bright Star asked.

"He is powerful and has many spies who help keep him in power. Many of their people are refugees from the north who fled fighting. Now they find themselves in a war with people many of them have never heard of. The problem for us is that he is obsessed with taking our lands, and he has more than ten-tens of tens of warriors. It will be difficult getting him isolated on a battlefield."

"How does he feel about witches?" Bright Star asked, smiling.

That led to a detailed description of how Bright Star and her sister lured their enemy away from his warriors.

White Fox listened but understood little of what was said. Her strong tea and pain made her drowsy to the point she collapsed against Bright Moon's shoulder. Red Hand helped Bright Moon get White Fox settled onto a sleeping pallet next to Bright Moon's bed platform.

The prisoner settled into a routine of giving lessons in her tongue to Bright Moon every day, then helping as much as she could around the longhouse with daily chores. She could not haul water or wood, but she helped prepare meals, cleaned up after meals, and helped some with small children. Her leg was getting a little stronger each day, and Willow Bark found she could change the poultice less frequently.

Bright Moon could not believe how quickly the Haudenosaunee tongue came to her. In less than a moon, she and White Fox could carry on a conversation. At the same time, White Fox was quickly learning the Monongahela tongue. The two were becoming very close.

When the cold maker arrived with strong winds, and bitter cold temperatures, Bright Moon decided

White Fox need not sleep on that cold pallet on the floor. She shared her bed platform where the two young women could share their body heat to stay warm. Being so close with just light sleeping dresses on led to a mysterious intimacy Bright Moon did not understand.

Bright Moon felt her body warming in places she had never felt before just watching White Fox strip her buckskin clothing off before putting her fabric sleeping dress on.

*What is wrong with me? These feelings are for others, not me! I want no part of intimacy. But I look at her body, and I want to feel her against me. I do not understand. I am NOT two-spirit...or am I? Is that why I cannot stand men? When White Fox and I look in each other's eyes, there is a connection there. I can feel it. No, it cannot be true.*

It was cool enough in her chamber that Bright Moon was happy to slide under the double elk hide blankets and pulled herself up against White Fox's back. Bright Moon's nipples were hard in reaction to the cool air. She felt them press into White Fox's back and enjoyed the sensation.

"Bright Moon?"

"Yes?"

"Do you wish me to roll over so we can be face to face?"

"Is that what you want?"

"I do not know. I have been intimate with boys

and warriors, but never another woman. I do feel a strong attraction to you. What do you feel?"

"I am very confused. I have never wanted anyone in my bed. Now, I feel you belong here. I do not know what I want. Does that make sense?"

"Yes." White Fox whispered, then put her hand on Bright Moon's at her side and pulled it up and over until White Fox's breast was under Bright Moon's hand.

Bright Moon felt her hand clench on the fullness of White Fox's breast. A tingling sensation spread through her body, her nipples hardened against her friend's back, and a warm, wet feeling emanated from her loins. She pushed her pelvis up against White Fox's butt.

White Fox rolled over so she could face Bright Moon. They wrapped their arms around one another and pulled their supple bodies together. Both women were in a place neither had been, nor ever expected to be. Bright Moon pushed a powerful thigh between White Fox's legs until she could feel the heat in her most private place. White Fox responded by humping against Bright Moon's hot crotch.

"I want to feel your skin against my skin," White Fox whispered with desperation in her voice.

"Yes..." Bright Moon whispered a needy response. They separated long enough to remove their sleeping dresses, then meshed their bodies back together.

Legs fully entwined, an arm around the other's back, and a hand squeezing one another's breast, they looked into each other's shining eyes in the dim light filtering through the longhouse smoke holes. White Fox pushed her lips to Bright Moon's.

Bright Moon had not kissed a person on the lips since she was a small child. The effect was like a beaver dam burst open. Wetness flowed from her eyes, her mouth, and her woman hole. She pulled White Fox harder to her body, squeezed harder on her breast, and pushed her woman parts harder against her newfound lover. White Fox reacted in kind while she pushed her tongue into Bright Moon's mouth.

The fire in Bright Moon's loins became an uncontrollable raging inferno. Tongues deep in each other's mouths, fingers rolling hardened nipples, and wet crotches rubbing together brought both to a seismic climax.

Completely out of breath and still clutching each other, no words came. After recovering her breath, Bright Moon brushed her lips against White Fox's. The passion was on again and just as hot as before.

"I have never known anything could feel like that," Bright Moon gasped to her lover.

White Fox slid her hand from Bright Moon's breast and trailed it down her sweaty, muscular stomach. When her partner's light fingers did not stop at her navel, Bright Moon began to wonder what else her newfound lover had in mind. She soon found out as those tantalizing fingers explored their way through her mat of black pubic hair, over her sensitive mound, then through her cleft, around her tingling folds, and finally entering her once-again heating woman hole. Her world seemed to concentrate on those dexterous fingers as they twisted and turned while she squeezed them with muscles she did know she had.

Her world moved faster as White Fox's finger slid in, out, and all around in her suddenly craven sex center. She moaned her pleasure as those fingers penetrated her, and her hips thrust again and again. Suddenly, rainbow colors flashed in her clenched eyes, her hand clasped onto White Fox's firm breast and hung on for life as every muscle in her body contracted around those magic fingers that held her life in their grip.

Finally able to relax, Bright Moon felt warm and satiated from head to toe. She leaned over White Fox and let her hand trail down her friend's body. Finding the places that White Fox had found on her, Bright Moon repaid every sensation. When the girl finally reached her shuddering peak of pleasure, she fell limp under Bright Moon's arm. Withdrawing her hand from that magic place, she returned it to White Fox's breast and gently massaged it. She bent down and softly kissed her lover on the lips and slid her body to White Fox's side.

"I feel completely happy and satisfied for the first time in my life," White Fox whispered to Bright Moon.

"Me too. I do not know where we go from here,

but I cannot imagine a happier place than right here, with you!"

"I do not think there is a better place. Are we wives? Husbands? Neither? What are we?"

"Happy. Let us leave it at that. I want to wake up with you in my arms."

Bright Moon woke up to the smell of corn gruel and spruce needle tea. Her eyes popped open, and she found her naked body plastered to White Fox's. She was warm and could smell the sex they had shared last night. She hugged her friend awake and asked, "Are you ready to face my family? I am sure we made enough noise last night to entertain everyone in the longhouse."

"If you can face them, I am sure I can. I never considered myself two-spirit, but after last night, that is all I ever want to be. Even more, I want to be your partner for the rest of my days."

"Are you sure? I have a war to fight in the spring. Many people will die. I pray to power that you are not one of them."

"Let us concentrate on getting through this day. Tomorrow will take care of itself."

"Agreed. We better get dressed."

When they walked up to the central firepit, all eyes were on them with many questions begging for answers.

"Good morning, young ladies," Bright Star opened the conversation.

Bright Moon dished a bowl of gruel and handed

it to White Fox, then got her a cup of tea. Then, she served herself.

"Good morning, everyone." Bright Moon addressed the entire family. It was unusual to see Water Mint, Tallow, all of their adult children, and three grandchildren at morning meal at the same time. Red Hand sat with his arms folded across his red war shirt.

"Do you have anything you wish to talk about this morning?" Red Hand asked with tight lips, as if he was ready to explode.

Bright Star gave Bright Moon a mother's supportive smile but said nothing.

"As you know, White Fox has been teaching me the Haudenosaunee tongue. I think it is obvious we have grown close. Last night, we decided to sleep in the same bed since it was so cold in my sleeping chamber. Our combined body heat would help keep us warm."

Water Mint's youngest son, ten and six sun cycles Oak Shield could not stop himself from snickering loud enough for all to hear. Everyone looked at him with daggers in their eyes.

Bright Moon smiled and continued, "When we snuggled, we realized just how close we had become. We talked and decided we felt right in one another's arms. I guess you heard the rest."

"I am happy for you, my daughter. This life is hard enough. A life partner makes it tolerable," said Bright Star.

Water Mint raised her teacup on a shaking arm. "I salute the Water Plant Clan's newest couple!" Her advancing age was more evident than ever.

"Do you wish a formal clan wedding, or do you consider yourselves already married?" Bright Star asked.

"Two-spirit weddings are very rare and are a great honor. We know you have great spirit powers, Bright Moon, and I presume power brought you together. A clan that hosts such a union is truly blessed," Water Mint added.

"I hope you have not forgotten that there is a war to fight in the spring, and your partner is a member of the enemy people who will be at our doorstep to wipe us from the earth." Red Hand said and looked around for support. He found none.

"We will do what needs to be done, War Chief," Bright Moon answered her father.

As the winter wore on, the Water Plant Clan and New Long Pine Village grew accustomed to having a two-spirit couple living among them. Bright Moon intensified the training of archers and one-on-one combat training.

White Fox asked Bright Moon to train her in the skills that would allow her to fight at Bright Moon's side in the upcoming war. Bright Moon doubled her efforts to bring her spouse up to speed. There was no talk of one holding back while the other fought. They would be equals on and off the battlefield.

## CHAPTER 13

# LITTLE RED

Winter progressed in Tall Ram's winter camp. The camp was on the south-facing slope low on a mountain. Elk, big horn sheep, and mule deer passed through the nearby pine and aspen forests, depending on weather conditions. Red Petal was among three young women who would be birthing their first child before the winter was over. All were anxious to put the blessed event behind them. All were quite aware of the dangers involved with birthing a child in the winter moons in the mountains.

Red Petal tried to stay active through the cold months, but many times heavy snows and blizzard conditions kept everyone in their skin and brush wickiups. After those confined times, it became more and more difficult to get up and move around. She was getting nervous about the delivery of her baby.

She had thanked every spirit she could name that she did not become pregnant when the evil chief had raped her. Now she was praying every day that she would deliver Redbone's baby healthy and happy.

She believed the baby would come at the end of the Starving Moon or the beginning of the Moon of the Spring Equinox. It was normally a bad time to have a baby due to the poor health everyone was in due to heavy winter snows. And this year had plenty of snow, but there were several thaws. Each thaw, Tall Ram's hunters were able to catch elk, bighorn sheep, and mule deer on the move. In the late fall, they had killed three grizzly bears, including the one Redbone was in on, that provided sufficient tallow to see them through the winter.

Now, as the days were beginning to get a little longer, she began to feel a little more confident. Her confidence took a hit, however, one day when one of the expectant mothers was working on scraping an elk hide when she tripped over a buried sapling. Her foot caught, and she fell onto her swollen stomach. Her weight snapped the sapling and the sharp point of the base of the small tree punctured her belly right into her birth sac. The loss of the birth water caused her to go into premature labor, and the child was stillborn. The entire village mourned the loss of the infant. Then the wound in the mother's belly was invaded with demons, and she lost her life, as well. Late winter was a somber time in Tall Ram's camp.

The equinox was marked by the arrival of a major blizzard that dumped upward of ten and two hands of snow across the mountain range. The only reward was there would be plenty of snow to melt for water. Red Petal became depressed with the forced inactivity.

But shortly after the snow stopped, the warm winds began to blow. Redbone watched the snow disappear nearly as fast as it had fallen. The high, open meadows were the first to become snow free, except where dips and gullies blocked the winds. Two days after the warm-up started, Red Petal went into labor. She had a large support contingent with a pair of midwives and others to help with any problems that might develop.

She was blessed with a labor that lasted only five hands of time on a warm day. She had the afternoon to rest and get her strength back. The child was a boy who had a shock of thick, black hair, dark eyes, pudgy cheeks, and pink skin.

"What will his name be?" Meadow Dew asked.

"His child name is Little Red. He will be a trader, like his father."

"I know you said you were not worried, but I was glad to see he had all the normal parts, and no extras. And he seems to be hungry," Meadow Dew added.

"Just like his father, he likes to suck on these." Red Petal gestured to her breasts and one exposed nipple.

That was when Redbone came into the lodge. "Looks like he is getting his fill! Is he whole?"

"Yes, my husband, just as I told you he would be."

"What did you name him?"

"Little Red for his child name. He is a little Red Petal and a little Redbone, so he is Little Red."

"You continue to amaze me, wife. I love you both!"

"You better! Do you want to hold your son?"

"Not now. I do not want to interrupt his first meal!"

"I love you, too, my husband."

"Can I bring you anything?"

"Just an uninterrupted night of sleep. But that probably will not happen until he has seen four sun cycles, and by then, another one will be waking me up at night."

"I suppose."

Two nights after Little Red was born, Red Petal fell into a deep sleep. Redbone kept Little Red occupied so she could get her sleep.

*Red Petal stood on the archer's platform along the palisade at New Long Pine Village. She had a bow in hand and a double quiver at her waist that held over two tens of chert-pointed arrows. Standing next to her was a beautiful young woman she did not recognize, but when War Chief Bright Moon came by checking on the readiness of her archers, she stopped and kissed the young woman and said, "For luck, my love."*

Soon war cries could be heard beyond the palisade wall. Bright Moon called out, "To your positions! Your loved ones are depending on you! Shoot straight. All of you are capable of cutting down the enemy before his archers are in range. Ready yourselves!"

Every archer turned to face the enemy, including Red Petal. She had never seen so many warriors. They were massed to attack New Long Pine and Black Bear Villages. Tension was on every face.

Suddenly, Bright Moon, the woman who had been at Red Petal's side, and two tens of warriors carrying bows walked toward the enemy. Bright Moon carried a white cloth, seeking a truce.

A large enemy chief, similarly escorted, walked out from the ranks of his warriors. Bright Moon and the Chief met and bowed to one another.

Bright Moon's words came to Red Petal's ears as if she was standing right next to her. "Chief Skanatego, I am Bright Moon, War Chief of New Long Pine Village. In the tradition of our long-passed ancestors, I challenge you to fight this war one-on-one with me. The fight will be to the death using war clubs and knives. If I prevail, your warriors will withdraw from this battlefield and never again try to occupy this river valley. If you prevail, Black Bear and New Long Pine Villages will leave this valley never to return. Do you accept these terms?"

"Ha! Before I kill you, I will take you as a slave and make you my personal concubine. Other than that, your terms are acceptable to me." Chief Skanatego gave her a

140

*predatory smile that said he was fully confident in himself.*

*The warriors formed a circle around Bright Moon and her enemy.*

Red Petal woke up to Redbone tapping her shoulder. He was holding Little Red, who was screaming. She took him and placed him at her breast. He fought to find her nipple and suckled frantically for a few heartbeats before settling into a more leisurely feeding.

Redbone noted she was wet, and he could smell her fear sweat. "Are you well, Wife? Did the evil chief enter your dream again?"

"I am well. The dream was about your sister. She was War Chief of New Long Pine Village. I was one of her archers. We were on the palisade wall facing many tens of tens of warriors. She marched out and challenged the enemy chief to fight to the death to end the war. He agreed just when you woke me up. I am worried about her and all your family."

"My guess is she knows what she is doing. But I know of no enemy that is a threat to our people."

"The chief's name in the dream was Skanatego."

"I never heard that name before. Maybe it was just a bad dream." Although he did not believe that.

"There is something else." She paused and looked down at the baby on her chest. When she looked up, she had a "you are never going to believe this" look on her face.

"What is it?" Concern was evident on his face.

"Your sister was walking down the line of archers. There was a very pretty woman warrior standing next to me. Bright Moon stopped, kissed the woman on the lips, and said, 'For luck, my love.'"

"Are you sure? Maybe you misunderstood her words."

"I do not think so. The woman looked back at her like I look into your eyes. And that same woman was at her side when she confronted the chief. Has Bright Moon ever said anything to make you think she is two-spirit?"

"Never! Well, other than she has always maintained she is not interested in any emotional attachment to anyone, especially men."

"How do your people feel about two-spirits? Are they accepted, shunned, or something in between?"

"No, they are honored. But most I have ever known about were women in men's bodies. They have acted feminine and usually become healers. I have never known a situation where two women were involved. Leave it to Bright Moon to do something no one else has ever done before."

"Perhaps, as you said, it was only a silly dream. But I worry that things could be bad for our family. If we went there after the spring thaws, we would not get there at least until the Green Corn Celebration. Of course, the war in my dream could be sometime in the future."

"What of the way we feel about these mountains? Are you ready to abandon this country?"

"If we go back there to check on everyone and introduce Little Red, we could come back here the next summer. We are good at traveling."

"We have a few weeks to think about it." Redbone ended the conversation, but he was far from finished thinking about Red Petal's dream.

# CHAPTER 14

# WAR PREPARATIONS

All through the winter, Bright Moon kept all the New Long Pine and Black Bear warriors preparing to meet a huge Haudenosaunee army as soon as the weather allowed river and overland travel. Using information provided by White Fox, a strategy was beginning to take hold in her mind. Secrecy, stealth, and luck would be the key components of her plan. She would not be able to share her plan until the last minute, and then only with a special party of participants. Her father would not be part of that party. Even White Fox would not know of it until it was time to execute, if she proved worthy of being on the team.

Bright Moon had six tens of archers who she had built special bows that would shoot arrows faster and further than warriors typically carried. Those bows would only be used from the shooting platform along the palisade. This would enable her archers to fire on the enemy long before they could shoot back. Along the shooting platform on the palisade were placed special baskets with five tens of the special longer arrows to be used in the long-range bows. Reserve supplies of those arrows were stored in each longhouse.

The ground would be too frozen to accomplish another idea she had. She wanted to dig a trench twenty paces out from the palisade. The trench would be eight hands deep and ten hands wide, then covered with a weak framework disguised under a layer of old leaves. When the enemy warriors approached with ladders to scale the palisade, they would fall into the trench, creating total confusion for several heartbeats. During those confused moments, her archers would launch a deadly fusillade of arrows. That plan had to be scratched because there simply would not be time to get it completed between the ground thawing and the expected attack.

Instead, she had teams working on lashing a framework of hand-thick limbs ten hands wide and running the length of the palisade about twenty paces from the wall. The frame would be laid on the ground and covered with a thin fabric. The entire frame would then be covered with a layer of old leaves. When the enemy warriors rushed to the palisade, their feet would break through and get tangled in the framework. Again, the resulting confusion would give her archers time to lay down a deadly fire.

Along the shooting platform near the top of the palisade would be large bladders of water for extinguishing any fires the enemy managed to start along the walls. More water bladders were set along the tops and bases of the longhouse walls.

Ten days before the equinox, Bright Moon considered her overt plans for the fight with an overwhelming number of enemy warriors to be ready. The archers from both towns were well practiced and as good as could be expected. The warriors without bows would be held in reserve behind the palisades of each town and sent to plug any breaches opened in the walls.

Three nights before the equinox, Bright Moon and White Fox went to their sleeping chamber early. The entire longhouse was treated to the unrestrained cries of two women making passionate love well into the night. It was after midnight when Bright Moon finally settled into White Fox's sweaty side to drift off to sleep.

*Bright Moon was sitting cross-legged next to a fire ring in a mountain forest. Snowbanks were common around the loosely organized village. A chunk of butt from some mountain animal was roasting on one side of the fire. On her right side was Redbone, then Red Petal holding a sleeping infant in her arms. Next to Red Petal was a young woman with a familiar face. Her belly was* swollen with a child. A handsome young warrior sat next to her.

"So, you have had a baby, I see," Bright Moon said to Red Petal.

"Well, not yet, but any day now. I know it will be a boy, and his name is Little Red. And who is this with you?" her sister-in-law replied.

"Glad you asked! Meet White Fox. She came to help me learn the Haudenosaunee tongue. Now we are married. White Fox, meet my brother Redbone, his wife, Red Petal, and their soon-to-be-son, Little Red. I do not know this beautiful maiden, but I see she is with child as well."

"This is Meadow Dew and her husband, Running Ram. She is the daughter of the trader, Sheep Talker, and he is the son of Tall Ram, chief of this village."

"Glad to meet you all!" Bright Moon said.

"Is there trouble at home?" Redbone asked Bright Moon.

"Yes. A Haudenosaunee chief named Skanatego plans a great war against us after the snowmelt runoff is gone. Sometime in the Planting Moon we expect."

"Can you get back in time?"

"Yes, we will be all right. I have a plan worked out, thanks to White Fox." She leaned over and kissed her on the lips.

"How long have you known you are two-spirit?" Redbone asked Bright Moon.

"I did not know until White Fox came along."

"And I did not know until I was until Bright Moon

*rescued me from my old life and let me see by a new light," White Fox added.*

*"Sounds like quite a story." Red Petal took up Redbone's hand. "We know about strange love stories."*

*"Yes, our family is rife with unusual stories, is it not?" Redbone said as he looked at everyone around the fire pit.*

*"I suppose the meat and tea are ready. We should eat. When do you need to start back?" Red Petal asked as she awkwardly stood up with Redbone's help. Suddenly, the baby was back in her tummy.*

*"Oh, we cannot stay. Red Hand is expecting a report on our preparations at the council meeting tomorrow. I am glad we found the time to visit. It smells delicious, though." Bright Moon replied, then noted everyone start to fade.*

*"We will be coming home this summer," said Redbone quickly.*

Bright Moon was awakened by White Fox's still swollen lips.

"We should go get cleaned up. We smell like last night," White Fox said with a mischievous grin on her face.

"Hmm. Maybe we should play one more round of that game," Bright Moon replied as she dragged White Fox down beside her and kissed her deeply.

Nearly a hand of time later, the young women walked up to the firepit in the Water Plant Clan long-house. They were clean and had clean buckskin war shirts and leggings on. Most of the clan kept their own firepits. Only Bright Star and Water Mint's families used the central firepit. Bright Moon motioned for White Fox to sit, then she did.

"I had a dream this morning. White Fox and I were visiting Red Petal and Redbone. She will have a baby within a few days. She said it is a boy named Little Red. She talked like he is already born, but said he would make his appearance in a few days. Just as we were leaving, Redbone said they would be coming home this summer. My guess is they could not get here before the Green Corn Celebration. We will see."

"We have a war to win before we can make any future plans," Red Hand said tersely as he looked into Bright Moon's eyes.

"Yes, we do, Father. Today, I need to check the progress of the "tripping frame" around the palisade walls. Also need to check with the arrow makers. All the strong bows are ready, and the archers are as good as they are going to get. I need to check the status of all the water bladders at Black Bear Village and here."

"Slow down, daughter. You need to make sure someone checks on all those things. You do not need to do it all yourself." Bright Star jumped into the conversation.

"I am just making sure she knows what needs to be done and that she is not letting distractions get in the way of the tasks ahead. This will be a war that requires our...her undivided attention." Again, Red Hand looked into Bright Moon's eyes, then to White Fox, who looked down at her half-eaten gruel.

Without arguing, or even acknowledging Red Hand's insult, Bright Moon asked Bright Star, "Are those long spools of fine sinew ready yet? We will need a team of volunteers to go string them through the forest soon. They will not stop our enemies, but they will slow them down and frustrate them, maybe enough to make some vital mistakes."

"Cool Dawn says the spools will be ready tomorrow," Bright Star replied.

"Father, can you think of anything we are missing?" asked Bright Moon.

"Yes, about five tens of tens of warriors to match the enemy's," Red Hand answered coldly.

"Fast Hawk should be back from Monongahela Village in the next few days. Hopefully he will have good news from Corn Silk."

"Are your archers committed enough to face an army two or three times, or more, larger than ours?

"Gray Dove and Elkhorn both say our people are ready to face the Horned Serpent if need be. But until they actually face the enemy, we cannot readily predict what will happen."

Bright Star smiled at the wisdom her daughter exhibited.

Of course, none of these people knew about the risky plan Bright Moon had put together. No one knew about it yet.

Bright Moon looked at White Fox. "Are you ready to get this day started?"

"Ready as ever."

"Let us go see how those trip frames are coming along."

After Bright Moon and her partner left, Bright Star looked angrily at Red Hand. "Are you jealous, Husband? Do you begrudge your daughter expressing her passion toward her mate?"

"She is not a mate! She is a...well, I do not know what you call her. A mate is someone you have children with."

"Is that it? Your daughter has chosen a partner who cannot give *you* a grandchild, and now you are upset? This is the first time I have seen my daughter happy since before her first moon. I am thrilled for her. And you should be happy about the good fortune this two-spirit union will bring to our family, our clan, and our village."

"Yes, well I am looking at an army three or four times the size of ours coming after us. Somehow that does not sound like such great fortune to me."

"And nothing has happened yet. Perhaps it won't."

———

A SECRET PLAN began to form in White Fox's mind. *It kills me to think my beloved Bright Moon even considers that she has a chance against Father's forces. He has too many warriors. He will kill her as sure as the sun comes up each day. He sent me here to spy on her and get him some answers that will make the destruction of her people inevitable.*

*I did my job, right up until I seduced her. How was I supposed to know I would fall in love with her? She is a perfect person. I cannot betray her, but I see no way to save her either. Perhaps I could go to him, convince him that her village is not worth what it will cost to take it.*

*If he will not listen, maybe in his bed, I can convince him to leave these people alone. He always tells me I am his favorite lover. Kill him before he goes on his war walk. I know I would never be at her side again. Humph, I would probably be killed for taking his life. So what? At least she would be safe. That means more to me now that I know her. No, I cannot kill Father. I must convince him.*

*I will volunteer to lead the team stringing the sinew trip lines in the forest. I will convince Bright Moon I am the logical one to do it. I know where to put them and how many. I can just slip away while we are doing that.*

---

THE BUDS on the trees began to open. The forest burst into light green and yellow colors as the deciduous trees began to flower. Countless birds began their courtship rituals with a cacophony of songs. Deer, elk, and moose began their calving season. Small animals of every kind began bearing litters of pups or kits. In short, the forest was alive with new life and the promise of more on the way.

Around the eastern forests, women began

preparing ground to plant the three sisters. Optimism for a new growing season prevailed on every tongue.

It was also the time for war. Fighting needed to be finished in time to get those three sisters (corn/maize, beans, squash/pumpkins) planted.

With fear of a great army descending upon them any day, Bright Moon was leading the preparations for the defense of Black Bear and New Long Pine Villages. Arrows were made and stored for quick access, bows were tested and retested to ensure their readiness. Other preps were ready or nearly so. It was the day she would send a few of her trusted warriors out to string sinew trip lines in the forest east of the two villages. Her White Fox, Gray Dove, and Elkhorn would lead a small party in setting the trip lines in overlapping rows between various trees in an arc some five tens of tens of paces out from the palisade walls.

White Fox tied off one end of her line to a small beech tree and told Gray Dove, the closest member of the party, that she needed to go behind some screening bushes to relieve herself. Gray Dove shrugged and trailed off to the north stringing her sinew line a hand above the forest floor. It was known that this was merely a delaying tactic meant to slow and frustrate the enemy.

When Gray Dove had moved more than one hundred paces away from her, White Fox slipped around a white cedar thicket and started her long trek for Ganeco Village. Hopefully, Skanatego would not start his war walk before she got there. She set her pace at a ground-eating trot that she could maintain for hands of time. She angled northeast crossing high ridges and descending into low valleys. It was hard work getting up the steep hills and difficult navigating swampy bottom lands.

She knew the trails that would take her to the Mud River. Hopefully, she would find a canoe to steal once she made it to the river.

On her sixth day, she reached a ridge that overlooked the bend that took the Mud River northwest. She was a day ahead of her planned schedule. She spotted a single line of a smoke rising next to the river. If her luck held, she would be in a canoe moving downriver to Ganeco Town within two hands of time. So far, she had avoided contact with any people. She had a normal hunting bow rather than the good bow that Bright Moon helped her craft. Her father did not need to know about that bow. She had only killed one turkey and was able to save that arrow. She mostly ate the jerky from the Water Plant longhouse stores she had taken when no one was looking.

White Fox stealthily approached the camp on the south riverbank. She spotted a single, small dugout pulled up on the bank. It was late morning as she moved from tree to tree looking for people. There was at least one person here to tend the fire. She saw a wickiup made of woven saplings lashed to a wooden framework and covered with cedar bows. It was little more than a lean-to.

When she got close, she could hear a man snoring in the small lodge. Bow at the ready, she walked into the camp. Peering around the wall of the wickiup, she saw the man laying on a sleeping pallet. He was gray-haired and carried little meat on a boney frame. He wore only a ragged, gray breech-clout with no designs. A raccoon skin was stretched on a hoop next to his relaxed arms and laying on his lap. A small scraper lay on a floormat close to his right hand. Apparently, he was scraping the hide when he fell asleep. An unstrung bow stood in a corner with a quiver holding six arrows. She decided to see if she could steal the canoe while he slept.

She was just out of bow range when she heard a shout. She looked back and waved at the old man. Maybe she would see him in a few days after she convinced Skanatego the Ohi-yo River was too far. The cost in lives and expensive attempted raids that he had already incurred did not occur to her. If it had, she would have realized her current attempt to convince him not go on his planned war walk was not going to end well.

———

FROM THE SHOOTING platform along the palisade at New Long Pine Village, Bright Moon anxiously watched a group of warriors walking in from the east. The group divided and about half started for Black Bear Village. They were too far to recognize individuals yet, but none stood out as her lover. When they got closer, she could see White Fox was not among them. She hurried down and when to the palisade opening to greet them.

Gray Dove gave her a grave look. Tears swelled in Bright Moon's eyes. When Gray Dove got close, she called out in a quavering voice, "What happened?" She remembered her station and stiffened, resolving not to look weak in front of the warriors. She could grieve later when she was alone.

Gray Dove shrugged and answered, "We really do not know. Everyone was working their own lines. I was close to her. I watched her tie a line to a beech tree. She said she had to go behind some bushes to relieve herself. I thought nothing of it,] and strung my line off to the north. That was before lunch. I went back to find her for noon meal, and I could not find her. Her spool of sinew was on the ground next to the beech tree she tied it to, but she was nowhere. I called and called.

"Eventually, everyone gathered around. We decided to search for her, but we found no tracks. The dry forest floor made it difficult to find anything. Turkeys had been everywhere. You know how they disturb the leaves. It looked like tracks everywhere, but we found no moccasin tracks other than a couple right there by that beech tree."

"Did you see any enemy tracks? Could she have been taken?"

"I do not know. We found no signs of a struggle, no blood, no tracks, no nothing. We even circled far to the east and found nothing. We searched all afternoon. Some of us will need to go back and finish stringing trip lines because we did not get finished today."

Bright Moon found it difficult to restrain her emotions, but she managed. "You others can return to your homes. Gray Dove, would you mind giving your report to my father?"

"Of course not. I will follow you."

"I am coming," Elkhorn spoke out as Bright Moon turned away. She spun around and angrily shouted, "No!"

He started to respond but thought better of it.

At the firepit, Bright Star and Water Mint looked at Bright Moon with deep sympathy as Gray Dove recounted the actions of the day. Red Hand kept his questions professionally on point, but underneath, he was skeptical. He had never trusted White Fox, believing she was a spy all along. In the Water Plant Clan longhouse, he held a minority view and kept his mouth shut as he looked for clues to support his view. She was good at hiding any ulterior motives.

After Gray Dove's report, she was dismissed. They ate a quiet evening meal. Bright Moon just swirled her spoon in her stew. Afterword, Bright Star put her arm around Bright Moon's shoulder and walked her to her sleeping chamber. The first thing Bright Moon saw was White Fox's sleeping dress. She picked it up and held it to her face, drinking in the scent of her lover. She burst out crying, holding nothing back. Bright Star held her tightly to herself and let her daughter cry it out.

Several times in the night, Bright Star awoke to hear her daughter crying in her bed chamber. Each time she started to rise, Red Hand would stop her.

"Leave her be. She needs to work this out herself. I just hope my own fears do not materialize."

"And what are your fears, husband? My daughter is lying in there devastated over the loss of the only love she ever had, and you want to talk about *your* fears?"

"My fear is that White Fox, if that is her name, is on her way to report to Skanatego exactly what defenses we have set up to fend him off."

"You think she is a spy? This whole thing has been an act? Do you believe she was able to fake all the passion she shared with our daughter? Our daughter who is so insightful, she can see her brother's actions all the way to the Shining Mountains? Yet, she cannot detect a fake lover in her own arms?"

"Have you ever faked your passion, just to get me to the end of mine so you could get to sleep?"

"That is different. You are not Bright Moon!"

Silence.

"By the spirits! You may be right! What do we do now?"

"Humph! What can we do? Bright Moon has worked out the best strategy for this situation. We are going to be greatly outnumbered, and now the enemy knows our strategy. Her long-range archers will need to be flexible enough to go where they attack first."

Naturally Bright Moon refused to believe the woman she trusted with her heart would deceive and betray her. But she did consider that White Fox had been taken by Skanatego's scouts and may have been coerced into revealing the defensive plans for the two villages. Each day they practiced shuffling the long ranges bows to different places along the shooting platforms. There was little else they could do.

## CHAPTER 15
# TRAITOR

White Fox timed her arrival at Ganeco Town for the dark of night. She slipped through one of the small gates made for women when they went to tend the fields. She was silently making her way around the base of the palisade when two strong arms wrapped around her chest. One hand went to her breast, the other covered her mouth, quieting any protest she might offer.

"Welcome back, Mink. You have been gone a long time." A confident male voice sounded in her ear. "If you agree to whisper when you talk, I will move my hand." She bobbed her head in agreement. He moved his hand from her mouth but kept the strong grip on her breast.

She wore a thin, dark buckskin shirt with long sleeves and dark leggings so she could move without being seen in the dark. Somehow Eagle Claw had seen her and snuck up on her. She was impressed.

"What are you doing? I must get to Father, I have much to tell him." she turned her head and whispered in his face.

"I will escort you to him. He may be occupied, which is what I have planned for you after you deliver your report."

"We will see."

"I caught this mink slinking around the palisade, Chief." Eagle Claw announced when Skanatego invited them into his chamber in the largest longhouse in Ganeco Town.

"It took you much longer to return than expected. I hope you have valuable intelligence for me. I would hate to have to punish my favorite spy." Skanatego said calmly.

Mink shrugged Eagle Claw's arm from her shoulder, gave him a menacing look, and turned back to Skanatego. "I have much to tell you, Father, but only for your ears. Please excuse this warrior so you and I can get down to business."

"I will send for you when I am ready, Eagle Claw." Skanatego waved a bare arm to dismiss the big warrior who was chief of Skanatego's personal guards.

Jealousy filled Eagle Claw with rage. The chief was going to couple with his own daughter, depriving him of his well-earned pleasure. He stomped from the chamber and left the longhouse. He did not need to hear Mink's cries of passion.

"Join me, daughter, your report can wait until we are satiated." He held back the blanket, revealing his naked body and engorged manhood.

*I can do this. After all, Father taught me how to use my body for so much more than copulation. I need to coax him not to go on this war walk. Eventually, I will tell him my souls have gone two-spirit, and Bright Moon is now the owner of my heart. But first I must turn his mind from killing her.* The thought spun in her head while she slowly, sensually disrobed for her father.

He had introduced her to the pleasures when she had seen only eight sun cycles. Then he just used light touches with his long, delicate fingers. She never knew her mother. The woman had died giving her life. Father doted on her like a grandmother as long as she could remember. She always slept in his bed, even when he had entertained one, or more, of his many mistresses.

Over the seasons, he touched her with increasing intimacy, always explain the rightness of his touch. By the time she had seen ten sun cycles, he was penetrating her little woman hole, showing her how good it felt. He knew just how to make her moan. At that time, he introduced her into providing pleasure to a man. He showed her how and where to touch a man. By the time she had seen ten and two sun cycles, he began sliding his manhood partially into her. After a few such experiences, she was begging him to push deeper into her. He also showed her how a man could pleasure her with his mouth, using lips and tongue. By then, he had her giving him the ultimate pleasure with her mouth. With his coaxing, she learned to like the hot spray of his essence in her mouth.

Once she was familiar with all the forms of fornication, he taught her how to use her skills to get the things she wanted. How to elicit information from a sex-drugged victim, how to distract an enemy using her wiles and bury a stiletto in his heart while she clenched his manhood with her special woman muscles, how to distract a handful of warriors as her friends performed some necessary war mission. Her techniques and uses for her body were endless.

After reaching her pleasure pinnacle three times (at least she convinced him of that), he lay down beside her and asked, "So, what intelligence do you have for me, my dear."

"Before, I tell you anything of that nature, I have something of great importance to tell you, Father."

"What is it child? You know you can ask me anything. I did note that you were distracted this time. Tell me and we will work it out, together."

"Happy to hear you say that, Father." She paused, cleared her throat, and began, "Father, I must ask you to cancel your war walk against New Long Pine Village and Black Bear Village..."

"What!?" He sat up and looked into her eyes in the weak orange light of the coals in the firepit.

"Those villages are filled with people who just want to raise their crops and families. They are not aggressive. They have no designs to expand their territory."

"May I remind you they have killed many of our warriors and scouts, including friends of yours?"

"They have only killed anyone in defensive actions. You have attacked them repeatedly, and they have defended their homes. Look at it from their position. They have never attacked any of our villages. Just leave them alone."

"What are you not telling me? I can see something behind your eyes."

"All right, I will be honest with you. You sent me to spy on the woman warrior. To find out who she is and how to kill her. So, I went there. I got wounded, by the way. That took me longer because I needed to heal. Anyway, being close to her, I learned what a fine person she is." A tear leaked from her eye. "Father, I fell in love with her. For the first time in my life, I experienced real love. The maiden and I shared our souls. We even married. I want her in my bed for the rest of my life. I am through sleeping with people, including you, to gain something. With her, we share each other, and that is more rewarding than anything in this world."

"I see," he replied calmly. He looked up at the smoke hole and noted a grayness in the sky—a new day was starting. The war walk would begin in two days. His daughter would be a problem, a problem he would handle in his special way.

"Guards!" he yelled. Instantly, three large warriors entered the room. "Bind and gag this woman and leave her in my bed. Find Eagle Claw and send him here."

"You have crossed the line, my daughter. I taught you how to use your body as a weapon. There is no room for 'love' in this world. I have also taught you loyalty. Apparently, you have forgotten that lesson. When Eagle Claw gets here, I will give you a lesson in loyalty. Eagle Claw is faithfully loyal to me. I will give you to him while I watch. If you learn, you can prove it by giving me pleasure with your mouth. If you cannot, I will consider you a risk to run. Therefore, Eagle Claw will cut the tendons in your heels. That will slow you down. You will also be at my side when New Long Pine Village is wiped from the face of the earth. You will watch your lover come to a most disgraceful end. How many warriors will she experience before her souls flee the wreckage of her body?"

Mink/White Fox sobbed uncontrollably. "How could you be so cruel, Father?"

"Do not talk to me about cruel, daughter. You are the only person I ever loved. And now you betray me. ME! You will pay the price, and so will your perverted lover. No one, not even Mink, betrays Skanatego. You will learn the hard way."

"I will die as 'White Fox,' Mate of New Long Pine

Second War Chief. I am no longer 'Mink,' daughter of the evil Chief Skanatego."

"So be it."

"My chief, you sent for me?" Eagle Claw called from outside Skanatego's chamber.

"You may enter, Warrior," Skanatego replied.

Eagle Claw walked it pensively. The first thing he saw was Mink laying naked on Skanatego's platform, tied to the frame spread eagle. Liquid oozed from her woman hole.

"You will take her, now, while I watch. If she does not demonstrate loyalty, you will cut her ankle tendons. That will discourage her from running. She will accompany us on a litter on our war walk. We leave at daybreak, two days from now. Be at it."

"Chief, I am not sure...with you here and all..."

"Do it, and do not worry about being gentle."

*I should never have come here. Bright Moon will die a horrible death while I am forced to watch. I do not think I can bear that.* She turned her thoughts inward as the big warrior began taking off his weapon belts.

When Eagle Claw grunted with his final thrust into the unmoving woman on his chief's bed, she simply looked to the side, holding her tears back. There was no pleasure in it for him, but plenty of pain for her.

When Eagle Claw pulled himself off her listless body and started to dress himself, Skanatego approach from the side. He was fully erect with a demented gleam in his eyes, a crooked smile on his lips.

White Fox's eyes were still closed, her head turned to the side. He pushed his hardened manhood against her soft, emotionless lips. She looked up at him with hate and started to turn her head. He grabbed her forehead and pushed her mouth against the tip of his erection.

"Your souls are loo..." she started to say when he forced his hardness into her mouth. She relaxed her jaw and opened her mouth wide to make as little contact with him as possible. He pushed himself into her throat, triggering her gag reflex.

"Make it difficult if you like, it will still happen," he said harshly as he pushed deeper into her contracting throat.

Her eyes bugged out as she fought for a breath of air. She clamped her mouth shut, digging her teeth into the tender skin of his penis. Her mouth flooded with the salty, metallic taste of his blood.

He withdrew from her mouth as quickly as he could, then drove a fist into her eye. Her world went black.

# CHAPTER 16
# BATTLE

Two tens and two days after White Fox disappeared, Bright Moon could not be found anywhere in New Long Pine or Black Bear Village.

Red Hand sent runners to every corner of both villages, but they came up empty. "She knows how critical this time is. Where can she have gone?" he asked every person he knew.

Water Mint suggested she may have gone hunting a spring bear to ensure her medicine was strong enough to be able to defend the villagers from Skanatego's army. That made no sense to Red Hand.

Bright Moon confided only in Gray Dove that when she was certain everything was in place, she would be out of sight. She was going to a secret location where she knew she would be in position to hurt the enemy the most. After she was gone more than a day, Gray Dove should report to Red Hand and

Fast Hawk what she knew and not to worry about her.

––––––––

REDBONE, Red Petal, and Little Red were loaded and ready to shove their canoe into the Sweetwater River. Red Petal had been having a series of bad dreams about Bright Moon and New Long Pine Village. They vowed to their new friends among the Sheepeater Shoshone that they would be back, but they needed to find out about the trouble at home. It would probably take until the Green Corn Celebration to get there. Most likely, any trouble will be passed by then, but they felt compelled to go.

They would trade along the way, maybe stop to witness the splendor of Cahokia again. The day was cool but sunny with light winds from the west. They would have their hardships along the way, but they could not ask for a better start. The hard part of packing their trade goods and personal belongings from Tall Ram's winter camp to the Sweetwater was behind them.

From there, they would be traveling downriver all the way to the Spirit River. But it would take them about two moons to make it from the mouth of the Spirit to New Long Pine Village. All they knew was Red Petal's troubling dreams, but those dreams had been accurate in the past. They were on their way to get some answers.

"WHAT DO YOU MEAN, 'A SECRET LOCATION?' Where, what location?" Red Hand demanded.

"I am sorry, War Chief. She would not disclose where she went. She said to tell you not to worry about her."

Fast Hawk listened carefully to every word Gray Dove said. *I know where she went. Spy Mound, she called it. From there it would be possible to watch the progress of the fight. But why would she take herself out of the fight? She said she knows Skanatego will kill White Fox. The only love of her life is gone forever. Wait! There is a place just upriver where Spy Mound can be seen. As we were coming by there, after going to the old Black Bear Village site, she said an enemy could set up a command center on that hill and watch the battle unfold. If an expert bowman was set up on the north side of the mound, he/she could deal the enemy a deadly blow.* "Cut off the head of the snake," she said.

He listened to Red Hand rant some more.

"If she has gone to try to find that lover of hers, at a time like this, I will make her wish she never came back!" Red Hand pounded his fist into his open palm.

"I hope you really do not mean that, War Chief. No one has done more to get this village ready to fight a war than Bright Moon. Has she ever let us down? No!" Fast Hawk was pushing Red Hand too hard, and he knew it.

"You are right, Fast Hawk. I just wish she would

confide in me. After all, I am her War Chief and her father."

"And you also know that she always does the right thing," Bright Star added.

*I am going to help her, but I will tell no one. If I take my small canoe upriver past Black Bear Village a hand of time to Mahoning Creek, I will be in position to move up the north side of Spy Mound I may be there in time to help her clear Skanatego's guards so she can get to the 'Snake's Head.' I need to get ready.*

When Fast Hawk arrived at the Deer Clan longhouse in Black Bear Village, he found his few belongings outside the door hanging. He pushed his way in and saw White Flower talking with Light of Dawn and Cool Dawn. As soon as the women saw him, Light of Dawn and Cool Dawn separated themselves from White Flower, but kept dark, steely eyes on him.

"What is it, White Flower? What have I done?" Fast Hawk asked.

"Nothing, that is what you have done. You have been so preoccupied with Bright Moon and this 'maybe' war, you have completely ignored me. I think you are still in love with her, so I am stepping aside. You can go back to her."

"But I was never with her. She would never allow me to get close to her. You know that."

"Well, in your dream last night, it sounded like you were very close to her. Yes, I mean intimately close. And that was after you had been intimately close to me! Well, I am finished, and so are we! I have already talked to Leaping Wolf of the Wolf Clan. He will be courting me in the future. You go back to your own village."

"But..."

"Go!"

He went out, gathered his things, and left Black Bear Village. *I guess I have nothing left to live for, so, come on Skanatego, let us fight!*

Three scouts ran into New Long Pine Village, and three more into Black Bear Village before the first light of the new day. All the scouts reported large numbers of enemy warriors coming from the east through the forest. In the dim starlight, they appeared painted for war.

The alarm went up, and all warriors took up their assigned positions, including the three tens of warriors each for Black Bear and New Long Pine Village sent by Corn Silk from Monongahela Village. All but two, that is. Missing from the palisade shooting platform at New Long Pine Village were Bright Moon and Fast Hawk.

Fast Hawk had paddled up Mahoning Creek for over a hand of time and had not seen or heard a thing. He came to a brush choked creek flowing in from the southeast. In the dark, he attempted to turn up the little creek. He came to an abrupt stop with a subdued "thunk." The sudden stop made him pitch forward, and the canoe wobbled, nearly capsizing.

*What?* Then he realized he had run into another

canoe. He struggled getting his boat stabilized enough to climb out in the deep water next to the steep bank. He managed to get his bow and quiver out of his canoe without getting the string wet, which would have been bad.

Once on the creek bank, he determined he had no place to hide his boat without making a lot of noise. Rather than leave it exposed for the enemy to find, he carefully tipped the short dugout to allow water to pour over the side. When enough water filled the hollowed log, it slowly sank to the murky bottom of the creek. He was able to hide a rope attached to the bow so that he could pull his canoe back to the surface, if he made it back to this creek. He quietly belted his double quiver around his waist, attached his war club, and checked his sheathed knife. It was still dark when he started up a trail along the creekbank that he hoped Bright Moon had followed.

Bright Moon waited just inside the tree line on the north side of the hill she expected Skanatego to use as his headquarters and observation post during the battle that he planned would be the end of Black Bear and New Long Pine Villages. With her long-range bow and arrows, she hoped to put an end to his plans.

Bright Moon had taken the memory of her mother's stories about the day Aunt Bright Moon had confronted an evil war chief more than two tens of sun cycles past. Her shirt, leggings, loincloth, and moccasins were all a dark gray color with random vertical black lines from head to toe. She had shaved her head and mixed charcoal and bear fat to make her face and head look just like her shirt. She even smeared the gray color on her bow limbs. She could stand in front of a tree and not be seen.

———

SKANTEGO'S WARRIORS left their canoes on the Mud River four days' travel west of Ganeco Town. From there they made their way west-southwest through rugged hills, several swampy swales and thick forest. The chief had decided the best attack would come from the east. Any attack from the Ohi-yo River would be too costly. The defenders could rain arrows down on them for hands of time before they could land and unload war canoes, just so they could begin their assault. From the forests to the east, they could get closer and arrange their assault in waves.

To the chief's bitter disappointment, their flotilla of canoes encountered a heavy spring storm that dumped enough rain to swell the river and creeks and render the swales into muddy bogs. The result was they were delayed more than half a day in their planned invasion. Morale among the young warriors was sinking.

When the multi-unit army finally encountered dry ground west of the storm's path, the anxious warriors were not to be slowed. In the bogs, several warriors simply faded away. The war walk was not what they expected. A full day before they would reach their objective, the first wave of running warriors fell flat on their faces after tripping over Bright Moon's sinew strings stretched across the forest floor. In the confusion, many clan units were broken and mixed with others. It would take many hours to sort out who belonged where.

After that first catastrophe, they no more than got started again when they hit another set of trip lines. After another long delay, they ran into more trip lines. Skanatego's great invasion force was slowed yet again. They were forced to move through the forest slower and more carefully. Morale among the warriors was sinking as they became more frustrated and exhausted. More warriors slipped away and headed back toward Ganeco Village.

Skanatego's unit with its ten-tens of warriors and elite guards were burdened with two litters. One carried Chief Skanatego and his current female companion, the other carried his helpless daughter, Mink, who lay on a blanket that covered the poles and skin covering that would be erected as a shelter for the chief. Mink was helpless because the big tendons connecting her calf muscles to her feet had been cut.

Her father considered Mink a run risk. He wanted to make sure she was at his side as they watched the destruction of her girlfriend's people. Bright Moon was to be brought to the chief where he could enjoy her slow death with his daughter. Perhaps then, she would learn loyalty.

Skanatego's party finally began filtering into the forest surrounding the prominent hill northeast of the New Long Pine Village palisade. The battle would begin a day after his plan, but Skanatego did not consider that a serious delay. His elite guards would scout and clear any enemies from the forest covering the north side of his observation post.

The black sky had just begun to turn gray when Bright Moon heard the first telltale sounds that indicated many feet shuffling through the forest litter to the east. She worked her way into the thicker cover close to the little creek that ran up the hillside toward where Skanatego would be set up. She needed to avoid them as much as possible, but would need to eliminate them silently, one at a time as the opportunity presented itself. White Fox had told her there were ten and five elite guards. At least half would be surrounding him. That meant seven or eight would be in the forest around her. There would be ten-tens of warriors between Skanatego and the battle to make sure no warriors escaped the battle and got near the chief.

Bright Moon was close enough that she could faintly hear the activity behind the palisade. She knew everyone would be taking their positions. She also knew there would be concerns that she was not there. Rumors would fly that she had abandoned her duties to run off with White Fox, who was an enemy.

She hoped Gray Dove, Elkhorn, and Fast Hawk, among others, would carry the day while she was cutting off the head of the snake—a plan that only she knew about.

As the sky began to lighten, from her position on the northeast part of the hill, she could see the first shadowy movements of the enemy heading her way. She watched a contingent of warriors carrying two litters to the top of the hill. *White Fox is on one of those litters. She is laying down. Why? Something is wrong with her!*

The litter bearers stopped. Bright Moon could see Skanatego and a well-dressed woman sitting at his side. The bearers just held that litter in place. A burly member of the elite guard walked up to White Fox, slid his arms under her shoulders and knees. When he lifted her, Bright Moon could see her lower legs were wrapped in bandages. She could see the pain on White Fox's face. *What happened? Why did she run? Before this day is over, I will know!*

A sound caught Bright Moon's attention. One of the guards was making his way up the hill behind her. She froze, hoping he would not see she was human among the tree trunks the same color as her disguise. The man walked by her less than two paces away in the dim, gray light. As soon as his back was to her, she stepped, reached around his left shoulder, gripping his mouth, and pulling her obsidian knife across his throat with her right hand. A hot liquid flood washed over her hand as he slumped to the ground. The tangy smell of fresh blood filled her nostrils.

After easing him to the ground, she looked around for another enemy. She spotted one down the hill to her right. He was moving downhill through thick trees. Suddenly, a hooded figure rose behind the elite guard, reached around, and slit the warrior's throat. The hooded man helped the guard slide to the ground silently.

*That looks like Fast Hawk. What, in the name of the gods is he doing here? He will get us both killed.*

A branch snapped across the little creek from her and downhill a short distance. She slowly looked and saw another elite guard making his way up the east side of the creek. She could never make it across the creek without being seen. Moving only her eyes, she watched him work up this hill until he was even with her position. *They suspect someone is in this forest. Hopefully none will live to call the alarm until I have lopped off the head of the snake!*

The warrior passed by her. She had a clear shot at him but could not get close enough to slit his throat. She would need to rely on a perfect bow shot. She raised her bow and aimed for his neck. He was about two tens of paces distant. She released her arrow. The projectile sped from her powerful bow and zipped right through his neck, barely slowing. She thought she had only wounded him, then saw streams of blood gushing from the entrance and exit wounds. He teetered and toppled over like a felled tree. Unfortunately, he hit the ground with a thump.

The big guard standing next to White Fox turned and saw the blood around the fallen guard's head. He called out something, and five more guards joined him as he rushed toward his fallen comrade.

Bright Moon sucked in a breath and took aim at the third man coming down the hill. She released and saw her arrow pass through the third warrior and stick in the gut of the one behind him. She could not get a clean shot at the big man bearing down on her, but she took out the one behind him.

Bright Moon had no time to draw another arrow, aim, and shoot, so she let her bow drop, pulled her war club and knife and waited for the big warrior to arrive. He already had his club pulled back and started a vicious swing as he approached her.

———

GRAY DOVE and Elkhorn stood at the ready on the shooting platform on the New Long Pine palisade. Along with eight tens of other warriors, they watched Skanatego's forces assemble in the dim early light of the most fateful day of their young lives. They were outnumbered at least four to one. There was no place to run. It was fight and die or surrender and die or become a slave. They would fight and die as they hoped everyone on that wall would.

Each archer had four tens of chert-pointed arrows within easy reach, and six tens of them held the long-range bows that Yellow Hair had shown their parents how to make more than two tens of sun cycles past. Only recently did Bright Moon, Yellow Hair's niece that he never met, actually build and test one of the bows. She was so happy with the results, she insisted all her archers use the weapons. They added more than twenty paces to the common bow's effective range over their normal hunting bows.

Gray Dove looked out at the enemy as they organized their attack. "It is a good day to die. We are outnumbered so dramatically. We do not stand a chance. And now we do not only not have Bright Moon to lead us, but Fast Hawk also went missing last night," she whispered to her new husband, Elkhorn.

"I thought you said she told you not to worry about her?" Elkhorn whispered back through the side of his mouth.

"That was before I stood here and saw all the enemy warriors facing us."

A shout reverberated through the ranks of the enemy warrior, and they started moving through the trees toward the palisade. The first two ranks of enemy warriors carried bows. Behind them, many ladders could be seen.

"All right! Let them have it! First volley, fire!" Red Hand shouted, standing in for the missing Bright Moon. He held the long-range bow that Bright Moon made for him. Six tens of arrows rained down on the enemy as they started to move. Six tens of enemy warriors fell, some dead, most wounded. The enemy continued to advance but were still far from their own bows' range. Six tens more fell. After the third volley, the enemy war leaders began to feel nervous. Their numbers were being rapidly reduced and had not been able to loose a single arrow yet. They were looking at the palisade and their warriors moving toward their objective. They never noticed a number of their warriors were slinking away from the battlefield from their rear ranks.

The Long Pine archers released their fourth arrow when the lines of enemy warriors began to falter. Fighters were dropping out of their ranks and retreating beyond the range of the New Long Pine archers.

As the enemy prepared to send yet another wave of warriors into battle, Gray Dove looked into the basket of arrows at her knees. A quick count revealed only ten arrows. Her heart sank.

"Elkhorn, we will not be able to repel another attack. We need more arrows." Gray Dove announced with little life in her voice. "And if the rest of our archers are as tired as I am, it may not matter. I do not know if I have the strength to draw this heavy bow one more time."

"Forget your complaining, we need more arrows, quick!"

"Red Hand! We need more arrows on the

shooting platform as soon as you can get them here! Hurry!" Elkhorn yelled down without even seeing Red Hand.

Gray Dove looked down the row of archers on the wall and saw many rolling their shoulders and stretching their backs. They were looking for reserves of energy anywhere they could find it. Then she looked out and saw the enemy forming and readying for a charge. "Get ready, people!" Gray Dove yelled. She had a sinking feeling that she would never give Elkhorn the son he wanted.

When the attack came, the archers shot arrow after arrow into the body of warriors coming toward them. At last Gray Dove reached for another arrow, but there was no arrow to take up. A tear came to her eyes as she watched the enemy advance. In a few more heartbeats, they would be within range of the enemy bows, and most of their archers had fired their last arrow already.

Suddenly new warriors arrived on the catwalk with baskets of fresh arrows. Just as the new arrows were almost to her position, someone yelled "Duck!" Gray Dove and Elkhorn dropped below the top of the wall as dozens of arrows flew over their heads. They grabbed the new supplies, loaded, and waited for the next volley to fly over their heads. They jumped up, loosed their arrows, ducked waited for more projectiles to fly by, jumped up and let loose another shot.

As if by some magic, the next time they stood, it

was to see the enemy falling back. What was happening?

───────────

BRIGHT MOON FELL BACK and rolled away from the charging warrior. He swung his club back the other way, just missing her ducking head. She jumped up, slashed her obsidian knife in an arc aimed at the underside of his club arm. Her blade cut deeply across his bicep and tricep muscles on the underside of his upper arm.

He roared and wrapped his left arm around her torso. She reacted by bringing her knife down hard into his thigh. He let her go and staggered back. He tried to swing his club with his weakened arm, but it was ineffective. Using her left hand, she slammed her club into his left arm, bruising deep into the muscles of his forearm. With him weakened and slowed, she slammed her club into his knee, sending him to the ground. Her next swing ended his life when her club came down on the crown of his head.

When she looked up, another of the guards was about to deliver a fatal blow to her head when an arrow drove into his chest from her right side. She looked up and saw a smiling Fast Hawk. She gave him a nod of acknowledgment and looked back up the hill.

Skanatego was standing and shouting something to his war chiefs. She saw her opening, stepped over, took up her bow, aimed, and released an arrow at his back. It was a long shot, but within the effective range of her bow. It struck into the lower right side of his back. Probably not fatal. Panic ensued at the field headquarters of Skanatego. Immediately the litter bearers picked up his litter and hurried off toward the east. The entire contingent of warriors accompanied their fallen chief.

The four war chiefs stood in a group dumbfounded. Their chief was down and gone, and they seemed confused as to what action to take. Their forces were in disorganized stages of retreat from the walls of both Black Bear and New Long Pine Villages. The ground was littered with dead and wounded Haudenosaunee warriors, and no one had found a way to penetrate the extra range of the special bows.

Taking advantage of the confusion, Bright Moon and Fast Hawk shot down two of the four war chiefs as they advanced on the headquarters. Bright Moon was anxious to get to White Fox so she could escort her to Willow Bark to treat her wounds. Her loyalty to her lover had not diminished.

# CHAPTER 17
# AFTER WAR

In a few heartbeats, Bright Moon stood over White Fox, who was sitting on a blanket with her back propped up. When the few remaining Skanatego warriors saw Bright Moon and Fast Hawk advancing with blood spattered faces and clothing, they dispersed into the forest to the east.

"Moon! I should have known you were behind this spectacle."

"Fox, we must get you to a Willow Bark!"

"No! It is too late for me."

"But..."

"Listen to me. I have much to say, and little time to say it." White Fox smiled at Bright Moon, but a painful tick twisted her lips every few heartbeats. "I know I really messed things up for us. I am so sorry about that. I thought I could save you. I was wrong. You could save yourself.

"Moon, I am so sorry. I am not who you think I

am or was. My given name was Mink. I never had a child name. My mother died in childbirth. I never knew her. Father raised me, and I slept in his bed from the day I was born.

"Father sent me to spy on you. He needed intelligence to decide how to crush you. I was to kill you, if I could."

"Wait, what are you talking about? You know I love you, and you love me. I know that."

"No, you understand nothing. White Fox was a made-up name I invented as part of my disguise. I was sent to assassinate you. And I would have, but I fell in love with you. Then I realized there was no way you could win against my father. He had too many warriors. I went back to try to talk father out of this war walk against you. I could not bear to see you hurt.

"I tried to tell him that I fell in love with you and there was no need for a war. Eventually we could form an alliance with Father and make our combined people stronger. But Father accused me of treason. He would not accept my new name nor my relationship with you. Then he said I was a risk to run away and had that big warrior you killed fornicate with me, then cut my heel tendons. I think after he made me watch you be tortured, he would have done the same to me. By then, he knew I would not turn my back on you."

"But he cannot hurt you anymore. No healer will

keep him alive with my arrow through his liver. I saw the black blood. His reign is over."

A painful expression wiped the smile from White Fox's face.

"Oh Moon, he has already killed me." A tear trickled from her eye. She used her eyes and chin to point to her stomach. A puncture hole showed in her blue-dyed doeskin dress. Black blood oozed from the hole. To her side but off the blanket was a long bone stiletto. "Father's weapon of choice. He used it after your arrow struck him in the back."

White Fox convulsed, coughed, gagged, and spit out a large, dark blood clot. She smiled up at Bright Moon with fresh blood on her lips. "Remember... the...love...we...shared..." Her eyes faded as painful cramps racked her abdomen. Slowly, her eyes fluttered as White Fox drew her last breath.

Bright Moon had already dropped to her knees and held her lover's hand as her life soul fled her broken body.

"I will always remember our love, and when I picture your beautiful face, I will smile," Bright Moon whispered to White Fox's fleeing life soul.

Weakly, she stood, tears streaming down her face. Her dark paint began to dissolve and run down her cheeks and chin. Fast Hawk wrapped his arms around her and held her as she sobbed into his chest.

After several heartbeats, she looked up at him. He had never witnessed such vulnerability in her eyes.

"Thank you for being here," she sobbed and laid her wet face against his bloody war shirt.

He held her for as long as she wanted. People started to gather around them, most from Black Bear Village since it was closer.

Fast Hawk heard someone say, "I do not believe they will be back anytime soon. They suffered horrendous losses."

From their vantage point, Fast Hawk could see most of the battlefield. The forest floor surrounding the palisades of both villages was littered with dead and dying Haudenosaunee warriors. He shook his head. *What a waste. All these souls sacrificed for one man's greed. How stupid!*

After standing there a hand of time, Fast Hawk asked Bright Moon if she was ready to return to her clan longhouse.

She looked down at the peaceful expression on the face of White Fox and started to say, "I would—" She was interrupted by a Haudenosaunee runner carrying a white wampum belt, signaling he was there in peace.

"War Chief, it is my duty to inform you that the Great Chief Skanatego wished the body of his daughter be brought back to Ganeco Town to be honorably buried next to him. He wishes to convey that he will not survive the trail back to Ganeco Town, but you, Great Warrior would be welcome and honored at the funeral."

Bright Moon stood there, feeling safe in Fast Hawk's arms. She was not able to respond.

"Tell your people..." Fast Hawk started.

Bright Moon cut him off. "Tell your people to send a runner to inform this warrior when and where the funeral will take place, and she will make every effort to be there. It will be an honor to walk among your people in peace."

"Long Strides will convey your message, Great War Chief."

"Bright Moon is Second War Chief, Long Strides. Make sure your people understand that. You may take the body." She dropped to her knees and kissed the corpse of White Fox on the mouth, smearing her lover's blood on her lips and Bright Moon's dirty paint on White Fox's pale face. "Goodbye, my love," she whispered before Fast Hawk helped her to her feet.

"One more thing, Deputy War Chief. Our warriors ask permission to retrieve our dead and wounded."

"Please do, but there will be no need for weapons."

"Yes, Deputy War Chief." Long Strides bowed his head and turned to give orders to his party. They placed White Fox on the litter and covered her with a blanket.

As the party carried the litter off, Bright Moon could hear gases escaping through the wound in the woman's abdomen. That was the last sound she wanted to hear from her beloved friend.

"Let us return to the Water Plant Clan longhouse and make our report. There will be many questions to answer."

"You are back!" Bright Star jumped up to greet her battle-weary daughter. Despite the blood, paint, and dirt smeared on Bright Moon's face, hands, and clothing, Bright Star wrapped her arms around her daughter and cried on her shoulder.

"You look exactly like my sister after she defeated an evil war chief. You made yourself up to copy her?"

"Yes, Mother. I thought it would give me some of her war medicine. I am relieved our archers carried the day!"

"Our archers did their job as you trained them. But going on that secret mission may have doomed us. Why did you do that the way you did? Without you here, those same archers may have been too demoralized to do as you instructed. Many thought you had run off to find your girlfriend," said Red Hand.

"Father, if I had said anything, many of our warriors would have tried to follow me, even if I had told them not to. Only Fast Hawk was foolish enough after he somehow figured out what I was doing. He managed to save my mission, and life, a couple of times in the bargain. I owe him more than I can say in words." She turned and looked at Fast Hawk, who was standing behind her, with promise in her eyes.

He returned a quizzical smile.

"So, you were able to cut off the head of the snake? We were not sure who was on that hill, but assumed he was the one wearing red. But we could see him carted off on a litter. We thought he was alive and well." Red Hand replied.

"Thanks to this warrior, I was able to put an arrow in his back. He stopped two others from getting to me. My arrow hit the chief in his lower back and damaged his liver and guts. He died after his guards carried him off the battlefield." Again, she looked at Fast Hawk with more than "thank you" in her eyes. He was confused.

"And what of White Fox? Did you hear anything about her?" Bright Star asked.

"She was right there next to her father. She was a prisoner, and he killed her after my arrow struck him."

"What? Her father killed her? I do not understand." Bright Star was stunned.

"Long, sad story..." Bright Moon spent a hand of time relating the sad truth behind her deceased love interest, including the complicated incestuous relationship with her father.

"Unbelievable! So, she was a spy. I was right about her!" Red Hand gloated. Bright Star's eyes shot daggers at him.

"In her words, 'You understand nothing!', Father."

"Care to enlighten me?" asked Red Hand.

"No! I care to go get cleaned up and sleep for a week." She took Fast Hawk's hand and led him from the firepit.

"Do you have any clean clothes, or are they all in White Flower's bed chamber?" Bright Moon asked Fast Hawk.

"My things are in a storeroom in the Hawk Clan longhouse. White Flower kicked me out because I called her Bright Moon in a moment of passion in a dream. She said she knew I was in love with you, not her."

"Do you still dream of me?"

"Yes."

"Good, that is one thing out of the way. Go get a set of clothes and meet me at the entrance of this longhouse. We have some things to talk about."

He stood there with a bewildered look while she retrieved a sleeping dress, light moccasins, and a woven grass basket from under her bed platform.

"Go! After we talk, I, we need some sleep."

Moments later, he met her at the entrance of the Water Plant Clan longhouse.

"Come with me," she said. She led him to the sweat lodge south of the Water Plant Clan long-house. Bright Moon started a fire in the small fire pit, then put some round rocks into the flames. There were already cedar needles a pot. She added some water and powdered mint, then slid the pot under the heavy hide cover of the sweat lodge. She started stripping off her filthy clothes and putting them in a pile, except her muddy moccasins, which she set off to the side. When she was naked, she took some soapweed leaves from the woven basket and slipped into the deep pool in the stream passing by the sweat lodge.

Fast Hawk followed her lead and stepped into the cold water and shivered. "S-so wha...what is g-going on? Why do you want me here?" He was just starting to adapt to the cold water. She was submerging, getting as much of the paint, blood, and filth from her shaved head as she could. Finally, she stood up, water dripping from places that caused Fast Hawk to forget about the cold water. She split a soapweed leaf and began working up a lather on her bald head.

"My deceased lover taught me how to love, Fast Hawk. But today, in the face of an overwhelming enemy, you taught me *who* to love. Yes, we saved our way of life, but you were out there to help me do a job that was critical to the future of our people. You were not told about my mission, not invited to join me. But you care about me enough to sacrifice yourself for my protection. All this time, I have been calling you a foolish one for caring about me. Well, today you made me see that I am the foolish one. I can see that, now." She stepped up to him and looked into his eyes in the dim, evening light.

Many clan firepits were sending flames and sparks into the sky. People were starting war chants and victory songs. Dancers were beginning to coalesce around the fires. The light from those fires shone in Bright Moon's eyes. Fast Hawk could see the affection in those dark eyes. He thought he would never be as happy as he was at that moment.

"Are y-you sure it is me you want, not the spirit of your deceased friend?" Fast Hawk asked timidly.

"She is right here in my heart!" She pressed her fingers to her chest over her heart. She stepped closer. "I am not sure I can make love so soon after... but I want you to know that I want to make you happy. I want us to be together."

"Bright Moon, I have wanted that since you had seen eight sun cycles. I could never get you to understand. Now, here you are, offering yourself to me, and I just do not know what to do. I fear that you will tire of me, and I will lose you. I could not bear that. You have always been my fantasy. Now, here you are, and I find myself afraid." He confessed.

"You showed no fear on that hill today. Today changed who you are in my eyes. You showed me strength I never knew you possessed. And you did it for me. I want to show you how much I appreciate what you did. But, more than that, I want you to believe what we can be. Does that make sense?

"Yes."

"Then come one step closer, kiss me, then take me into the sweat lodge."

The first contact between them was her cool, hard nipples against his muscular chest. His arousal was immediate. Then, their lips met, followed by tongues. She felt his hardened manhood against her stomach. She pressed her mouth and chest harder against him. After the long, passionate kiss, she dragged him from the water to the sweat lodge.

She lifted the lower end of the heavy hide cover while he used big wooden slats to lift hot rocks from the fire pit and drop them into the water pot in the lodge. Cedar and mint scented steam erupted from the water pot. She dropped the cover, took his hand, and led him into the low sweat lodge.

"I have never made love in a sweat lodge," he confessed.

"I have never made love to a man before, so this could get interesting," she replied.

The victory drums and dances went on until the sun rose the next morning. Except for the oldest elders, and the littlest children, Bright Moon and Fast Hawk got more sleep than anyone in the two villages. After their tryst in the sweat lodge, they snuck into the longhouse, saw no one, and continued into Bright Moon's bed chamber. Despite her plans for more lovemaking, when she lay on her elk sleeping skins, she was sleeping before Fast Hawk could pull her naked body close to his. He was a handful of heartbeats behind her. That was before midnight, and it was afternoon before either awoke.

When sun light peering through a smoke hole struck her eye, Bright Moon woke up completely disoriented. She discovered herself naked and plastered against Fast Hawk's back. She started to smile as the memory of their first lovemaking started to come to her. The urgency of her bladder changed her course of action. She slid off the bed platform, donned her sleeping dress, and headed for the piss hole behind the longhouse.

After she was gone, Fast Hawk woke up and had no idea where he was for a few heartbeats. Sweet memories came back to him, then he began to wonder where she was. His bladder signaled to him that he had to take some swift action, too. He put on his clean breechclout and was out the door.

It soon became apparent that the whole village was just getting moving. After the tumultuous events of the previous day, followed by a night of dancing, had everyone's schedule off.

When Bright Moon and Fast Hawk finally made it to the firepit, Bright Star and Water Mint were the only ones left in the longhouse.

"We missed you last night." Bright Star looked at Bright Moon, her eyebrows dancing in question.

"I had some things to do." Bright Moon answered vaguely.

"So I see," Bright Star said, eyes glaring at her promiscuous daughter.

"A new beginning. We have peace, now."

# EPILOGUE

Bright Moon accepted Fast Hawk as her husband in a formal clan marriage. She found herself falling deeper in love with Fast Hawk as each day passed. *How did I miss all the signs that he was the right mate to my souls? You needed White Fox to teach you what love is first, you silly loon!*

As it turned out, there was no funeral honoring Skanatego or White Fox. Although she was seen as a victim by some, when the investigation into Skanatego and his life exposed his incestuous relationship with his daughter, both were outcast from the Haudenosaunee. And their names banned from use by the people. When a runner delivered that message, Bright Moon stoically took the news in stride. "I honor her in my heart—that is enough," she told Fast Hawk.

At the Green Corn Celebration in New Long Pine Village, the child, Little Red, was introduced as the

Grandson of Head Matron Bright Star and War Chief Red Hand.

Redbone, Red Petal, and Little Red spent the winter in New Long Pine Village before loading their canoe with trade goods and setting out for the Shining Mountains at the beginning of the Planting Moon.

At the following Summer Solstice Celebration in Monongahela Village, Yellow Lotus was introduced. She was the first of four daughters, including a set of twins born to Bright Moon and Fast Hawk. At the same event, it was announced that Bright Star had stepped down as Head Matron of New Long Pine Village. Pretty Lotus, daughter of Water Mint was elected Head Matron by the Council of Elders. It was also announced that Red Hand had stepped down as War Chief of New Long Pine Village. The new war chief, due to overwhelming popularity, was Bright Moon.

New Long Pine Village and Black Bear Village remained the northernmost villages among the Monongahela people.

# BIBLIOGRAPHY

Appelt, Martin. "Man, Culture and Environment in Ancient Greenland," Publication No. 4, Danish Polar Center.

Bierhorst, John. *Mythology of the Lanape: Guide and Texts*. University of Arizona Press, 1995.

Bronsted, Johannes. *The Vikings*. Penguin Books, London, 1960, Revised 1965.

Clarke, Helen and Bjorn Ambrosiani. *Towns in the Viking Age*. St. Martin's Press, New York, 1991.

Cohat, Yves, tr. Ruth Daniel. *The Vikings: Lords of the Seas*. Gallimard, 1987

Damas, David. *Arctic, Vol. 5, Handbook of North American Indians*. Smithsonian Press, Washington, D.C., 1984.

Editors, Charles River. *Native American Tribes: The History and Culture of the Inuit (Eskimos)*.

Feasel, Charles T. *White Bear*. Ballantine Books, New York, 1990.

Fitzhugh, William and Elizabeth Ward. *Vikings, The North Atlantic Saga*. Smithsonian Press, Washington, D.C., 2000.

Gordon,E. V., rev. by A. R.Taylor. *An Introduction to Old Norse*. Oxford Press, London.

Gronnow, Bjarni. *Late Dorset in High Arctic Greenland: Final Report on the Gateway to Greenland Project*. Canadian Archeological Association, 1999.

Grumet, Robert S. *The Lenapes (Indians of North America)*. Chelsea House Publishing, 1989.

Harrington, Mark R. *Religion and Ceremonies of the Lenape*. Forgotten Books, 2012.

Harrington, Mark R. *The Indians of New Jersey, Dickon Among the Lanapes*. Rutgers University Press, New Jersey, 1966.

Heckewelder, John and Ernestus Gotlieb, notes by William C. Reichel. *History, Manners, and Customs of The Indian Nations Who Inhabited Pennsylvania and the Neighbouring States*. Historical Society of Pennsylvania.

# BIBLIOGRAPHY

Ingstad, Anne Stine et al. *The Discovery oy a Norse Settlement in America. Excavations at L'Anse aux Meadows, Newfoundland,* 1961-1968. Tromso, 1977.

Jones, Gwynne. *A History of the Vikings.* Oxford University Press, 1968, 1973, 1984.

Kunz, Keneva, tr., edited by Gisli Sigurdsson. *The Vinland Sagas.* Penguin Books, London, 2008.

McCullough, K. M. "The Ruin Islanders: Thule Culture Pioneers in the High Eastern Arctic," Archeological Survey of Canada, 141, Canadian Museum of Civilization, 1989.

McGee, Robert. *Ancient People of the Arctic.* University of British Columbia Press, Vancouver, 1996.

McGee, Robert. *The Last Imaginary Place.* Oxford University Press, New York, 2005.

Mcleod, William Christi. "The Family Hunting Territory and Lenape Political Organization," American Anthropology 24.

Maschner, Herbert, Owen Masson, and Robert McGee. *The Northern World AD 900-1400.* The University of Utah Press, Salt Lake City, 2009.

Maxwell, Moreau S. *Prehistory of the Eastern Arctic.* Academic Press, New York, 1985.

Means, Bernard K. *Circular Villages of the Monongahela Tradition.* The University of Alabama Press, Tuscaloosa, 2007.

Rasmusen, Knud. *Eskimo Folk Tales.* Gyldendal, Copenhagen, 1921.

Roesdahl, Else. *The Vikings.* Penguin Books, New York, 1987.

Schledermann, Peter. *Crossroads to Greenland, 3000 Years of Prehistory in the Eastern High Arctic.* The Arctic Institute of North America of the University of Calgary, 1990.

Seaver, Kirsten A. *The Frozen Echo, Greenland and the Exploration of North America, ca. A.D. 1000-1500.* Stanford University Press, Stanford, CA, 1996.

Simpson, Jacqueline. *Everyday Life in the Viking Age.* Dorset Press, New York, 1967

Sutherland, Patricia, ed. *Contributions to the Study of Dorset Paleo Eskimos.* Canada Museum of History, 2005.

Trigger, Bruce G. *Northeast, Vol 15, Handbook of North American Indians.* Smithsonian Institution Press, Washington, D.C., 1984.

# BIBLIOGRAPHY

Weslager, C. A. *The Delaware Indians: A History*. Rutgers University Press, New Jersey, 1972.

# A LOOK AT:
## RIDIN' WITH THE PACK VOLUME TWO: A WESTERN SHORT STORY COLLECTION (WOLFPACK PUBLISHING ANTHOLOGIES)

**Saddle up and venture into the wild frontier of the American West with Ridin' with the Pack: Volume Two, a gripping anthology that celebrates the timeless allure of Western storytelling.**

From rodeo circuits to deadly secrets buried in Montana grasslands, each story unravels a vivid tale of survival, justice, and redemption.

Readers will navigate the trials of a young veteran fighting to keep his family's ranch, a man haunted by his past on a quest for vengeance, a former outlaw struggling to leave behind his crooked life, and a Norse adventurer facing his fate on the shores of a newly established colony. Alongside these gripping tales, the search for a legendary pirate treasure tears apart a man's life, a family legacy built on grit and fortitude is threatened by an old frontier rivalry, and the desperate choices of a woman stranded in Dodge City lead to unexpected salvation.

In every tale, the spirit of the West shines through, each story unraveling like a chapter in the epic saga of the untamed frontier—where freedom, grit, and the unyielding quest for justice resonate like the timeless strains of a cowboy's humble heart.

Written by a talented crew of seasoned veterans and rising stars, Ridin' with the Pack: Volume Two showcases the enduring spirit of the classic Western tale.

Ridin' with the Pack: Volume Two features Western short stories by:

- Best-Selling Author B.N. Rundell
- Best-Selling Author Ken Pratt
- Award-Winning Author C.K. Crigger
- Award-Winning Author John D. Nesbitt
- Award-Winning Author Chris Mullen
- Award-Winning Author Harlan Hague
- Ron Briggs
- Nicholas Osborn

***AVAILABLE NOW***

# ABOUT THE AUTHOR

Ron Briggs is a veteran, having served four years in the USAF. His education includes a Bachelor of Science in Range and Wildlife Ecology at Oklahoma State University and a Master of Science in Range and Wildlife Management at Texas A&I University.

He is retired from the USDA-Natural Resources Conservation Service, and his career encompassed twenty-five years as District Conservationist in Linn County, Kansas. Prior to college, he worked seven years in the building trades.

Having developed a deep interest in history, especially in the pre-colonial period of North America, Ron's interests prompted him to begin researching a pre-history story about the Tallgrass Prairie Region of the Great Plains. That research evolved into his current multi-volume work, the Yellow Hair series, which includes scenes from northern Europe to the mountains of western North America.

Ron and his wife, Debbie, currently live in Mound City, Kansas, and have two grown children and seven grandchildren. His interests include spending time

with family, writing, hunting, fishing, traveling, and
woodworking.

www.ingramcontent.com/pod-product-compliance
Lightning Source LLC
Chambersburg PA
CBHW011517240626
47154CB00010B/3066